HEAD
CASE

Also by Bonnie Traymore

Killer Motives
Little Loose Ends
The Stepfamily

HEAD CASE

A PSYCHOLOGICAL THRILLER

BONNIE TRAYMORE

Interior and Cover Design by FormattedBooks

First Edition

Pathways Publishing
Honolulu, HI

Paperback ISBN 979-8-218-26461-1

For my readers

CONTENTS

PART ONE

Leave

Prologue	3
One	5
Two	15
Three	27
Four	32
Five	39
Six	45
Seven	54
Eight	62
Nine	69
Ten	76
Eleven	83
Twelve	87
Thirteen	93
Fourteen	101
Fifteen	107
Sixteen	112

PART TWO
Stay

Seventeen 119
Eighteen 126
Nineteen 131
Twenty 138
Twenty-One 145
Twenty-Two 149
Twenty-Three 158
Twenty-Four 164
Twenty-Five 169
Twenty-Six 175
Twenty-Seven 184
Twenty-Eight 188
Twenty-Nine 193
Thirty 196
Thirty-One 202
Thirty-Two 205
Thirty-Three 209
Thirty-Four 215
Thirty-Five 218
Thirty-Six 227
Thirty-Seven 231
Epilogue 235

Acknowledgements 241
About the Author 243

PART ONE

Leave

PROLOGUE

Kimi

Kimi knows what the other teachers call her behind her back. She's heard them before, although she's pretty sure they don't know she knows.

Here comes the mole.

It's not like she signed some formal agreement. And it's not like she had much of a choice. It had all started pretty innocently. Her boss befriending her and then subtly starting to pump her for information.

Then it became an unstated directive. A quick promotion to English department chair in exchange for some hints about who might be plotting behind the woman's back. Getting her preferred chaperoning duties in exchange for a few tidbits about who might be holding up her latest initiatives.

And then it became even more complicated.

She wonders how Brooke will take the resignation letter she left in her mailbox yesterday afternoon. It's a terrible career move to leave now, just two weeks before winter break. But Kimi feels that she doesn't have much choice.

It's not just the strained relationship with the other teachers, although that's part of it. It's that she's pretty sure her boss doesn't know what she overheard, and it needs to stay that way. She'll go back to North Carolina and regroup, then come back for the rest of her belongings some other time.

As she enters the deserted Cortlandt train station and starts walking towards the tracks, she feels a chill run up her spine. It's dead still on a frigid Saturday morning. No commuters. Not another passenger in sight. But she has a nagging sensation that she's not alone.

Is someone following me?

She stops for a moment and turns to look behind her. Nobody's there. She glances out the window to the parking lot, but the view is obstructed by a thin layer of ice. Then she takes a deep breath, steadies herself, and makes her way over to the staircase that leads down to the train tracks.

The hairs on the back of her neck are standing up, but she reminds herself there's a good chance she's overreacting—to all of it. And for a moment, she considers that she might be making the biggest mistake of her entire career.

Too late to second-guess myself now.

When she lifts her foot to start down the stairs, she freezes, reacting a split second too late to the sensation of a presence behind her. In an instant, she's flying headfirst in the air looking down at the cold, menacing metal stairs.

She closes her eyes and braces herself, incapable of emitting the terrifying scream that's welling up inside her.

ONE

Cassie

I accepted this position last summer, in the wake of a gut-wrenching breakup. You'd think after he broke my heart, he would at least have been gentlemanly enough to offer to move out of our apartment and let me stay put.

But that's not how it happened. He reminded me that it was his apartment first, which is true. Then he offered me a small sum of money. And then he gave me a deadline to find a new place. It was all very businesslike.

"There's someone else?" I asked.

"Does it really matter?" he replied. "What's the point in doing this to yourself, Cassie?"

He tried to deny it at first, to spare me the sordid details. But I eventually got most of the story out of him. We'd been living together for over a year. Dating for over two. I thought we were "going somewhere." Our sex life had never been electrifying, but it was satisfying and comfortable, and that was enough for me.

When things cooled off a bit, about six months before he dropped the bomb on me, I figured that was just how it was in a long-term relationship. I'd never lived with anyone before, so I had no frame of reference.

Then our silly little arguments stopped. He began to act polite—the way you interact with a relative stranger—like he didn't care enough to fight back. I felt something was up. Something had changed, but I didn't dare bring it up. I held my breath and waited to see if things would go back to normal.

I guess on some level a woman can sense when she's losing a guy, I just wasn't ready to face it. Because for me, getting involved with someone is a lot more complicated than it is for the average person. In hindsight, I suppose I can see that the relationship was never all that great. He probably did me a favor by ending it.

But it was all I had at the time, and I wasn't ready to let go. So when he told me that, yes, there was someone else, I felt like I'd been punched in the stomach. I have my pride, most of the time, but it seemed to be eluding me that day.

I'd like to say I held my head high and stormed out when he fessed up, but that's not what happened.

"You better be sure about this," I offered. "I don't give second chances."

"I'm in love with another woman. I'm sorry. It's over."

Then he turned from me and walked out the door.

So when I went to a conference in New York City the following week and learned about a teaching position at a boarding school thousands of miles from my California home that offered faculty housing, it seemed like it was meant to be. I could pocket my payoff from Evan, regroup, start over, and live happily ever after, following a proper but brief mourning period. I had just turned thirty so I didn't plan to pine away for too long.

Obviously, I wasn't thinking straight. I've stranded myself on top of a mountain in rural upstate New York, surrounded by acres of woods. A two-hour trek to New York City on a good day.

What was I thinking? Who am I going to meet here?

One thing I've learned from this experience is never make a major life decision in the midst of emotional turmoil.

I moved here from San Diego, totally unprepared for the insane winter weather we've been having here. Falcon Ridge Academy sits near the top of a medium-high peak of the Catskill Mountains on a plateau overlooking the Hudson River far in the distance.

It all looked so beautiful when I came to interview back in June. The day was clear and breezy, the setting a bucolic wonderland. I imagined long walks in the woods surrounded by vibrant fall colors where I would clear my head and heal my heart. A respite from the rat race. I'd write. I'd think. I'd grow stronger.

Now it's December, and the campus feels more like a minimum-security prison: isolated, creepy, and desolate. The walls of my four-hundred-square-foot apartment feel like they're closing in on me as the bare branches of the tree outside my bedroom window scrape at it with each gust of wind. Long, craggy fingers trying to claw their way inside.

From a distance, the structure I'm housed in seems to teeter on its foundation, threatening to tumble down the steep mountainside with every gust of wind. It's perilously close to the drop-off behind it. I was surprised that there's no real barrier there, aside from a row of stubby, round sage green shrubs that dot the perimeter of the grounds behind my building.

Winter arrived early, with a vengeance. And although the weather warmed up a bit today, there's still snow piled up outside from a "squall" last week. At least I'm learning some new vocabulary words. That's a blinding snowstorm that comes out of nowhere and makes it impossible to drive, see, or basically do anything, including walk from my apartment to the dining commons. I have no sense of direction. I'm sure I'll get lost and freeze to death or fall down the mountain before this winter is over. And it's just getting started.

Could this possibly get any worse?

But as I stare down at the alert on my phone, I realize I shouldn't have asked that question. They've called an emergency meeting of all faculty and staff that starts in twenty minutes. On a Sunday. And it's supposed to be my weekend off.

I thought we outlawed indentured servitude, but apparently not. For nine months of the year, they own me, and they know it. I forgo the primping—there's nobody to impress anyway—throw on some clothes, grab my jacket, and head out the door.

Kimi Choy is dead.

I heard our head of school say it, but it's not registering. I feel detached, like I'm watching a movie. I'm not sure if that's because I'm in shock or because I'm simply a terrible person. I was pretty close to her, at least until recently. Shouldn't I be feeling something?

Other people are reacting. I see a few eyes tearing up, but I can't seem to get my brain around it. The fact that this happened out of the blue. The fact that she was totally fine when I saw her Friday afternoon—and now she's gone. The fact that she died from a fall down the stairs at the Cortlandt train station.

Why did she go there, one of the most deserted stations around, and one that's at least twenty miles south of us? There are busier ones closer to our school she could have used.

And then I realize I'm probably in shock. I think back to when I arrived last August. Kimi was my department chair, and she went out of her way to make me feel welcome.

I'd never worked at a boarding school before, but she was a veteran. She was really friendly and offered some tips about where to get my hair cut and how to stay sane. She warned me that I would need to get some distance from the place on my weekends off. And she was really supportive when I told her about my break up and what a hard time I was having.

"I've got the perfect solution!" she said.

"What?"

"Let's go to the city for a night. Hit some of the trendy spots. Get you out there again."

"I don't think I'm ready to be 'out there,' Kimi."

"Oh, come on. It doesn't have to go anywhere. We'll get dressed up. Flirt a little. I could use some attention, too."

She had a point. Proximity to Manhattan was part of the reason I took this job. I love it there, but I didn't realize how hard it would be to get into the city.

"Okay. Let's do it," I said. What did I have to lose?

We had a great time. Shopping. Bar-hopping. Most of it by ourselves, but we did mingle with a pair of older banker-type guys who seemed to enjoy the company of two "hot teachers." It didn't go anywhere, and I suppose we could have been offended by the comment. I needed an ego boost, though, and it worked to lift my spirits.

Our friendship cooled off a bit over the semester, and that's on me. Other teachers warned me off her, saying she was a sycophant, in tight with Brooke Baxter, the Dean of Faculty and our supervisor. Anything I told Kimi would get back to her, and Brooke is the type of administrator you need to vent about on a daily basis.

And now I feel guilty for going along with the crowd, for not giving Kimi the benefit of the doubt. It's possible she didn't have a choice.

Because the other teachers were right. Brooke Baxter is, at best, a power-hungry narcissist who'll stop at nothing to get ahead. At worst, she's a full-on manipulative psychopath. The woman hasn't bothered me much yet, but then I stay as far away from her as possible, and I hardly present as the weakest member of the herd. I'll do my time, save some money, and leave.

If Brooke got her hooks into Kimi, though, she may have felt her only option was to go along. It's possible she sought Kimi out because of her diffident demeanor. Like all mean girls, she preys on the weak ones.

I abandoned Kimi and left Baxter free to feast on her. And now I feel terrible about it. Kimi reached out to me the other day, in fact. She said she wanted to tell me something important. I told her I'd check my schedule and get back to her, but I never got around to it. I could have made time, but I didn't.

I feel truly horrible. I was weak, but it's like *Lord of the Flies* around here. The isolation of this place combined with the close proximity to a limited number of other adults who were strangers to me just a few months before creates a surreal atmosphere. Fitting in matters more here than in any setting I've been in since middle school. Alliances form out of necessity, like a nine-month-long season of *Survivor*.

Thinking back on my behavior and the way I cooled to Kimi, I finally start to feel something. Tears erupt and stream down my face as I admit to myself that I was a coward and a total shithead to her. And now I can never make amends because she's gone forever.

My tender moment comes to a halt when two police officers enter the auditorium and walk up to our new head of school, Doug Walker. He seems just as surprised to see them as I am. My stomach lurches and I sit up straight. I feel a tingling in the back of my scalp as I struggle to process what's happening.

I turn to the person next to me, an older cafeteria worker named Sharon who always calls me "dear." Her eyebrows rise as we lift our hands and shrug at one another.

What are police officers doing here? This was an accident. *Wasn't it?*

———

I've been hiding in my apartment all day. I'm about to venture out to the gym, but I don't want to run into anyone. Our boarding population is pretty small, only about sixty students. They dine with us for lunch during the week, but they eat in their building on the weekends. Unless I'm on duty, I pretty much have the weekend to myself, and I don't see too many students, but it's impossible to avoid my coworkers unless I hibernate.

I know the gossip mill will be churning today. I'm not in the mood to engage, so I've been avoiding the other faculty members, which means I have nothing to eat besides cheese and crackers, the only food in my mini-fridge. I decide I might as well get a workout in before grabbing an early dinner, and I head out.

The school campus itself is fairly compact, less than a hundred acres, and houses several buildings. There's the dilapidated faculty apartment building where I live; the state-of-the-art student dorm and center on the opposite side of campus; the central, two-story building that contains the classrooms, gym, and faculty dining commons; and the executive residences adjacent to the central building.

Calling the architecture eclectic would be a euphemism. The central building is old-school Gothic, made of brick and stone, the student center is modern and sleek, and the faculty dorm sits on the edge of campus like an afterthought: shabby, not chic, and fit only for the help.

As I'm walking to the gym, my mind is reeling. Is it possible that Kimi's death was foul play? Why else would the police come to the school? It's not like it happened here on campus.

The administration offered no explanation for the police officers. They simply wrapped up the meeting and dismissed us, so we are all left to speculate. And what people dream up on their own is usually so much worse than the truth. I wish they would level with us, although they might have their reasons for keeping things quiet. Maybe the police tied their hands.

I start to consider the implications, and I feel like my blood pressure is a little elevated. There's an energy in the air that wasn't here before—morbid curiosity mixed with fear—and an undercurrent of grief for those with a heart. Nothing happens here most of the time. It's not like living in a city where sensational news bombards people on a daily basis. The thought of a murderer in the area is terrifying yet titillating for some people but not for me.

I don't like being in the limelight. I like to keep a low profile, and not just because I feel out of place here. If they open up a murder investigation and question us, they might start prying into people's pasts. That's not good because I have something to hide.

And it needs to stay hidden.

My attempt to avoid other faculty members failed miserably, but it ended up being okay. After my workout, I shared a dinner table with some other faculty members. The mood was pretty somber. Even the two biggest Kimi-bashers looked remorseful.

It was surprisingly comforting to experience a shared sense of grief, and I decide to stop being so negative. My attitude is probably part of the problem. A major reason why I'm having such a hard time adjusting to this place.

I vow that I'll try to give people around here more of a chance. It's too late to make amends to Kimi, but at least I can learn something from the way I treated her.

The wind has picked up again and the temperature has plummeted. I can see my breath as I approach my building. I pull my collar tight around my neck. I'll be happy to get back into my room, even if it's not that warm.

It's dark already although it's not very late, and I long for the California sun as I enter the deteriorating structure, walk up the creaky steps, and get safely into my apartment.

Once inside, I hear the scraping of the tree branches on my window. I make a mental note to email the facilities team tomorrow to ask them to cut back the trees, but I'm not going to hold my breath. Falcon Ridge Academy is in a death spiral in terms of student enrollment, and I feel like it's on its last legs.

The boarding program relied a great deal on international students, and although that market has bounced back a bit, it's nothing like it was years ago. Even before the pandemic, they'd started to accept day students in an effort to fill seats, but that only kept things at a subsistence level.

The campus is in Ulster County, on the opposite side of the Hudson River from the train line to Grand Central Station, in an unincorporated hamlet with the same name as the school. A hamlet is a small village with no governing structure. The closest town is Plattekill. We rely on them as well as other nearby towns for our municipal services.

I'd never heard of a hamlet before I moved here. Most people outside the state of New York probably haven't either. There are hundreds of them peppered throughout the vicinity. And it's apparently difficult to determine where many of them begin and end.

It seems very medieval to me, and I wonder what the implications are. What happens when we have an emergency? Do the various towns we rely on for ambulance or police service flip a coin for who comes? Most people don't seem to give it a second thought, so I keep these concerns to myself.

Although there are some pockets of wealth in the area, generally speaking, this isn't a very affluent area. Not many families around here can afford our tuition. As a consequence, we're struggling to stay afloat. That's probably why they keep it so freaking cold; I doubt there's much of a budget for tree pruning. I turn on the television, my only companion, get ready for bed, and count the days to winter break.

TWO

Cassie

I drag myself out of bed and into the bathroom after a fitful slumber that seems to have left me even more tired than I was last night. I should wash my hair, but I don't have the time.

Instead, I pin up my shoulder-length dark waves, enter the shower, and let the hot water run over me, trying to exorcise the chill that's nestled in my bones. I wash and exfoliate my face and scrub with citrus body wash to try to perk up my limbs. Letting the steam from the shower waft out into my bedroom, I towel off, hoping to warm up my apartment a bit.

I smooth some moisturizer on my perpetually dry face and take a good look at myself. I always thought I had an olive complexion, but maybe it was just the California sun. I have never been so pale. It's a stark contrast with my dark hair and eyes, so I apply some tinted foundation and stop to add a touch of mascara, which I haven't used since I've been here. If I'm going to be more social, I may as well look halfway presentable. I don't get carried away, though. Like I said, who am I going to meet on top of this godforsaken mountain?

"Hi, Cassie."

Ed Roberts, the tall, geeky, white-haired patriarch of the science department, waves me over to the empty chair next to him near the front of the auditorium, which can hold about two hundred people. With fewer than forty faculty and staff employed at the school, the space appears cavernous. I would rather have sat farther back, but I head over to him.

He's starting to feel like a friend, although he's old enough to be my father. They've called another meeting before school today, and I'm wondering if they are going to tell us anything more about what happened to Kimi.

"Hey, Ed."

"You look nice," he says as I settle in next to him. I feel maybe I should tell him that comments like that date him. I don't take offense or anything. It's just that younger guys seem to know instinctively not to give those kinds of compliments at work. Still, it's nice that my efforts are appreciated, even if it's by someone nearly twice my age.

"Thanks," I reply.

I take off my scarf and place it on my lap.

"How are you holding up? Weren't you close friends with her?"

This catches me off guard. I didn't realize people thought I was close with Kimi. I don't feel like I'm close friends with anyone at this place.

"I, um…" I clear my throat.

And now I feel like I'm being put to the test, like the ghost of Kimi is hovering over me, waiting to see if I'll throw her under the bus again.

"Yes." I give my head a nod. "She was a good friend."

Ed places his large hand on my shoulder and gives it a rub, and I look over at him. I heard his wife died about a year ago, and he's been having a hard time. His hazel eyes seem perpetually filled with grief, like a light behind them went out. I noticed it right away, although I didn't know the reason. He's always been kind to me, and I wonder if perhaps we bonded due to our shared sense of loss, although I can hardly compare my breakup to the death of his wife.

Doug Walker, our new head of school, is about to take the stage when Judy Prather sits next to me. She's the last person I want to see. She's the math department chair and perhaps the only woman at the school who could go toe to toe with Brooke Baxter.

She dresses like a secretary from the fifties: ridiculously high heels, body-hugging dresses that fall just below the knee, and poofy hair that looks sprayed into place. Judging from her face, she can't be more than late forties, but her outfits age her. And I don't know how she doesn't break her neck on the icy pathways that meander around campus.

Judy turns to me, leans in, and places a hand on my forearm. "Cassie. How are you holding up?"

I pull away from her, and my right shoulder bumps up against Ed's.

"How am I holding up?" My tone is sharper than I intended. I don't like her, but I shouldn't be so obvious about it.

"I mean, I know that you and Kimi were…close."

I narrow my eyes at her because she's the one who initially gave me the heads-up about Kimi being tight with our boss and suggested I cool off the friendship. She's playing a game with me.

She folds her arms, leans back, and shoots me a sideways glance.

I don't really want to make an enemy out of her, though, so I try to soften our interaction. "I'm shocked, like all of us. But thanks for asking, Judy. It means a lot."

The corners of her mouth lift up to a half-smile and she nods. Perhaps it's genuine. Then she looks off to the side, fiddling with a stray strand of hair. Maybe she feels like an even bigger piece of crap for bad-mouthing Kimi than I do for abandoning her. I certainly hope so.

We focus our attention forward as Doug Walker takes the podium. He's a tall, striking man in his early fifties with just enough gray popping through his dark hair to make him look distinguished but not old. The previous head of school was dressed down when I met him last summer during the interview process, as I've heard he was most of the time, but Walker is always in a suit and tie.

He seems well-liked by almost everyone, although it's only been a few months. Most people are on their best be-havior the first months after they start a new job, so it's hard to tell. There are rumors about a health problem. I have no idea if they're true. He looks pretty healthy to me.

"I want to thank everyone for the outpouring of support we've received and give you an update on the situation."

He goes on to tell us that the police being here yesterday was routine. At present, there's no reason to suspect that Kimi's death was anything more than a tragic accident. I feel relieved, and I'm happy to go back to my biggest worry being the fact that I was a shitty friend.

After a bit, he gives the floor to Brooke Baxter, Dean of Faculty, and our second in command. She looks harmless enough, but we all know better.

She's a smaller woman with a formidable stance. She wears her dark hair in a blunt cut that curls in towards her collarbone. The outfit she's wearing—slacks and wedge shoes with a white cardigan—makes her look a few years older than her actual age, which is somewhere around early forties. I sense that's intentional. She's a bit insecure about her youth and about managing so many people with more experience than she has.

I'm surprised when she takes the podium and announces that she's already found a replacement for Kimi. Who on earth would be available this late in the year for a position this undesirable?

Some guy named Dan Moralis, that's who. She gives us some background on him. He comes to us from an international school. He's returned to the area because of a sick grandparent in the vicinity. It's just before winter break, and the semester's not over yet, but he didn't want to wait a few more weeks to come home. I suppose it's touch-and-go with his grandmother and, lucky for us, he's available to stay through the academic year.

She continues with his credentials, and she's borderline gushing, which is weird. He has a master's degree, she says, but some of the faculty here have doctorates. A master's is sort of a given at an independent school. Especially in the humanities.

But then I guess in this job market, she's feeling fortunate to have any warm body to put in front of the students, never mind a qualified one. I take some comfort in that thought, and I hope it continues to be a teacher's market for a few more months until jobs for next year are posted. Then I can secure a new position and get out of here.

"I'm pleased to introduce you to Dan Moralis. Please give him a warm welcome."

Someone in the front row stands and walks up to the stage, and I suddenly feel grateful that I've brushed out my hair and slapped on some mascara for the first time in months. I can't believe my eyes. Dan Moralis is a total hunk. It's like a Christmas miracle.

I look down at myself. I'm wearing a navy sweater dress that flatters my curvy figure, with stylish yet practical waterproof boots, and I'm thankful this is the first day I don't look like a lumberjack. This guy could be a lumberjack though. He's wearing a long-sleeved black thermal shirt, almost the same color as his ebony hair. I can see his biceps and delts straining against the fabric.

Then I realize how totally inappropriate this is. First, I ice out Kimi, and now I'm swooning over her replacement. I'm not planning to act on these feelings. But I take it as a good sign that my heart is starting to heal, as well as some other parts of my anatomy. I'll do my time here, keep a low profile, save money, and go back to San Diego in June ready to put myself out there again. In the meantime, I have to say, the arrival of a hot guy on campus makes things a little more tolerable for me.

We all start to get up, like we're about to be dismissed. We're going to be late for first period if it doesn't happen soon. But then she starts again.

"Oh, and I have one more announcement. I've decided to promote Cassie Romano to English department chair. Although I must apologize if this comes as a surprise to everyone. Including Cassie herself. Hopefully, it's a pleasant one."

She gets some compulsory chuckles out of the crowd and dismisses us.

I look over in disbelief at Ed, and he flashes me a smirk. I've confided in him that I'm planning to leave, so I'm sure he knows this is the last thing I want. *So much for keeping a low profile.* I also realize that now my hands are tied in terms of Dan. I'll be his department chair, so he's somewhat off-limits. I know I just said I wasn't going to act on my attraction, but it was nice to have the option. Any fantasies I have of a steamy romance to keep me warm at night during this long, cold winter can stay safely tucked inside my head.

Brooke Baxter is divorced, and I wonder for a moment if she planned it that way. Promoting me to department chair so I'd be less likely to go for him, and she could have him to herself. I don't think she's stupid enough to hit on him, but then you never know. Smart people do stupid things for love all the time.

———

After an abrupt beginning, the rest of my day was pretty uneventful. It was busy though, and I didn't even have time to be introduced to Dan because the faculty meeting ran late and I had to rush to class. Brooke Baxter popped in on my first break to let me know we'd meet more formally tomorrow. And to make sure I was up for the job. And that I actually wanted it.

What could I say? Of course, I said I was fine with it. And I even pretended to be a bit grateful for the opportunity. I know I'm acting like a suck-up, but all I want is to get out of here. All schools want a recommendation from your previous supervisor. Brooke holds my life in her hands, and she relishes that fact, I'm sure.

After that, I got on with my day, taught my classes, and kept to myself. I didn't see Dan at all. Not at lunch, and not just now when I grabbed an early dinner. Most people eat later, and it was more deserted than usual this evening. I ate alone, which was fine with me.

On my way to my apartment, I stop to grab my mail from my cubby in the admin building. In with the junk mail and an issue of *Education Weekly*, there's a letter in a plain white envelope with "Cassie Romano" and the school address printed in block letters. There's no return address.

I find this a bit unsettling, and one step away from those bizarre letters you see in crime shows, with cut-out words pasted together to form a chilling message. But then I remember getting a few letters from religious groups back in San Diego. They were always addressed by hand. Maybe that's all this is. Still, how would they know to call me Cassie? My legal name is Cassandra.

I have a sinking feeling in my stomach, so I bury the letter inside my magazine and walk a little faster, enter my building, and head up the stairs. It seems strange that somebody would use snail mail these days to reach me if this letter is somehow important.

Continuing down the hallway to my studio, I check my phone to see if there are any text messages or voicemails I missed. But I see no new communications. I'll check my email when I get inside, and I make a mental note to check my spam folder too.

Then a blood-curdling scream fills the air—and it's coming from me. I've nearly run smack into someone. My keys and mail fall onto the worn beige carpet. Whoever it is seems about a foot taller than me, so I can't see whose face it is. I step back and look up. Of course, it's Dan the Hunk. And I just stand there.

Dumbfounded.

There are two studio apartments on this wing of the second floor, but the one next to me has been vacant all year. The presence of another human being near my apartment caught me totally off guard.

"I'm so sorry I startled you," he says.

Then he bends down and starts picking up my mail. The mystery letter is peeking out from inside the magazine, so I quickly crouch down and stuff it back in. But as I do, my hand lands clumsily on top of his, and things get even more awkward. It's like an electric shock goes through me. A delightful electric shock, and I wonder if he can tell.

Meanwhile, I still haven't said anything, and it feels like it's been way too long. I pull my hand away, grab my mail, and smile, but it's more of a clowny grin, not sexy at all. As we start to stand, I finally find some words to use.

"No, *I'm* sorry. I wasn't looking where I was going. But there's been nobody on this floor all year."

"Right. Sorry to invade your space."

He smiles, and of course he's got a totally sexy smile. Not blindingly white like a pretty boy, but white enough. If his teeth were yellow or chipped or missing, perhaps I'd have a fighting chance here.

"Not at all," I say.

"I just moved in. I guess I'm your next-door neighbor. I'm Dan." He pauses while I stare at him, still somewhat in shock. "Dan Moralis?" One brow lifts, like he's wondering if I even know who he is.

"Right! The new English teacher. I'm Cassie Romano," I say.

"You're the new English department chair. I suppose you're my...boss?" He holds out his hand and smiles.

We shake hands, and I try not to feel anything, but it's useless. He's even better up close than he was on stage. There's a faint manly smell emanating from him. I'm guessing it's shaving cream or deodorant because he doesn't look like the kind of guy who would bother with cologne. Or maybe it's just a man scent, something I haven't been around in a while. Although as I recall, Evan never smelled like this.

"Oh, no." I shake my head and let out an awkward, honking laugh. "Brooke Baxter's your boss. I'm just a paper pusher."

"If you say so."

There's another agonizing silence. I search for something clever to say, but I fail miserably. "Well, I'll let you get on your way."

"Nice to meet you, Cassie Romano. Have a good night."

"You too, Dan."

When I get inside my quarters, I close the door, bolt it behind me, and take a deep breath. After that painful interaction, at least I don't have to worry about the consequences of an illicit campus romance. I'm sure I've effectively ruined my chances. I'm totally out of practice after being in a relationship for so long.

I wonder for a moment why they didn't give him Kimi's apartment. Hers is much bigger. But then I remind myself that she's only been dead for two days. It's probably still got all her stuff in it. She was single, and I think about who will come to gather her belongings. Probably her parents. I decide I'll offer to help pack up her things. It's the least I can do.

In all the chaos, I totally forgot about the letter. I sit down on my tiny green loveseat, holding it between my thumb and forefinger. It's postmarked Plattekill, the closest post office to the school. I feel like I'm holding Pandora's box. I should just rip it up and throw it away.

But of course, I don't. I stare at it for a bit longer. Then I open it. I scan down to the bottom, and my fingers start to tremble.

It's Kimi Choy, talking to me from beyond the grave.

I read it carefully, twice, and I'm still not sure what to make of it. The letter is vague and fairly brief, expressing concerns that "something strange" is going on at the school and asserting that Brooke Baxter is out to get the new head of school, Doug Walker. She tells me that Brooke is angry that she didn't get the head of school job, something I already know. Everyone knows that. Why would she tell me that in a letter?

Then Kimi informs me she's going to resign. She warns me to be careful of Baxter and to watch my back. I wonder if she was planning to leave town that morning and never return. Maybe this is her way of saying good-bye to me.

I know the right thing to do is to give it to the police, but I don't want to call attention to myself. Besides, she didn't say I should go to the police if she was found dead. And there's nothing at all earth-shattering in this letter. Doug

Walker said there's nothing to worry about in terms of foul play, and I don't want them poking around in my business. I have no reason to think this was anything more than a tragic slip and fall.

Right?

We all know about the feud over the head of school position. It even spread to the board of directors. A board member even resigned in protest about the decision, one of only two women in the group of seven. Brooke expected to be promoted to head of school when the last one retired, and she and Doug were finalists for the position. It's common knowledge that she blew a gasket when they gave it to outsider Doug Walker. She threatened to file a lawsuit, claiming gender discrimination.

Doug Walker is the school's first African American head of school, but he's still a man, she pointed out, and then she gave the board a bunch of statistics trying to show that gender discrimination is more of an issue in private school administration than race. Which might be true—the stats on women in independent school leadership are terrible—but that's not the reason she didn't get the job.

She didn't get the job because she's a toxic administrator, and one of the least popular leaders I've ever worked for. She bullies people and plays favorites. Pits people against each other. And nobody wants to work for her. I'm frankly shocked they kept her on after her little tirade. I'm assuming it's because they're afraid of a lawsuit, and they're hoping she finds something else soon and moves on, as we all are.

I care less than most people because I'm out of here in a few long months. I sometimes fantasize that they fire me so I don't even have to finish out the school year. But they won't. And I need a good recommendation, so I'll stay on and do a decent job. And just in case there's some truth to Kimi's warning, I'll stay out of all the drama. Which brings me back to the letter and what I should do with it. What if it's important in some way? Is it fair to Kimi to rip it up and forget about it?

Then a thought occurs to me. I could send it to the police, anonymously. My fingerprints are all over it though, so I'll use gloves, cut off the part with my name on it, make a copy on my computer printer, and send it off to the police. Then, I'll have officially made amends to Kimi, and I can get on with my life.

THREE

Miles

"**W**hat the fuck is going on over there, Brooke?"

I realize a split-second too late that if I want information from her, this probably isn't the best way to get it. But she's been avoiding me, and I don't like being ignored. But I'm in my study, just a few rooms away from my wife and daughter, so I remind myself to keep my voice down.

"What do you mean?" she replies, with a hint of sarcasm.

"You know what I mean. I have to hear it on the news that this teacher of yours died? Why didn't you call me? And why didn't you return my phone call last night?"

"I didn't even know about it myself until early Sunday morning. I figured Doug Walker would call and tell you about it. Isn't that *his* job?"

Here we go again.

I made her all kinds of promises about the head of school position, promises on which I failed to deliver. But then I hadn't expected so much pushback from the other board members. I'm board chair at Falcon Ridge Academy, but I'm not a king. We hire by committee, and there were legitimate concerns about her management style.

27

I could throw that in her face right now, but I've got more to lose than she does at this point, and if she's becoming unhinged, she could even be dangerous to me. She knows too much, so I'm stuck having to play nice. I hate that she has something on me. But then I have something on her too, so I need to keep that top of mind.

Plus, she has a point. It's Doug Walker's job to inform me about the teacher's death, not her job. And if there's any chance Brooke's mixed up in it, I need to tread carefully. But I need to see her, to read her facial expressions and her body language.

I find it a strange coincidence that she voiced concerns about Kimi Choy being on to us just a few days earlier while I sat in this very chair using this very same burner phone—and two days after that call, the woman turned up dead. I'm losing patience, but I need to try and play it cool. Not let on that I'm harboring doubts about her.

"Doug did call me, Brooke. That's not what I mean, and you know it. But we need to talk. Are they doing an investigation? Did she say anything to anyone? Do we need to be concerned?"

"We shouldn't be talking on the phone," she says.

"It's my burner."

"Well, it's not *my* burner."

I realize that she's right about that too. Maybe I'm the one who's becoming unhinged. My back is against the wall and I'm running out of time, so I'm not thinking straight. We settle on a face-to-face meeting the following day at our usual spot: a clean, low budget chain motel just outside town. And then we sign off.

I come out of my study and make my way through the hallway, the foyer, and the living room. I stop when I spy my family in the dining area. I can smell something pungent coming from the kitchen, and I realize I'm hungry.

Garlic and ginger maybe?

But I see my wife Madeline helping our sixteen-year-old daughter with her homework at the dining table, so I assume the meal will take a bit longer. Our dog Max, an aging golden retriever, is curled up near my wife's feet.

Madeline gives our daughter a hint, but doesn't solve the math problem for her. Erin has a pained look on her face, and I watch as Madeline places her hand on our daughter's shoulder and gives it a rub. She looks over at her mother. What passes between them is timeless and precious and beautiful. There are no words exchanged, but I'm confident that Erin knows she's supported, and that her mother has her back. Erin takes a deep breath and goes back to work, and I see a smile light up her face when she comes up with the correct answer. But even if she hadn't, I'm sure she knows she'd be loved just the same.

Madeline makes it all look so effortless. Keeping our family on a steady course. And it puts my stomach in knots to know that it's all in jeopardy.

My wife's face is clean and bare today. I can spot the faint row of freckles that dot her nose and cheeks. I've always loved them on her, even more so now because I see them mirrored in our daughter, and I don't understand why she covers them with make-up. They make her look young. Fresh. Innocent. Like when we first met.

I've tried my best to be a caring husband and father. And up until recently, a solid provider. It's Madeline who keeps the family unit together, though. I love my wife and daughter very much. And as I take in the sight of the two of them, I'm thankful that they have no idea that their world is in danger of being blown apart—and I'd like to keep it that way.

There's still a way out, so I don't want to let on about any of it until the last possible moment. And even then, I'll do what I can to protect them.

Madeline finally notices me.

"How long have you been standing there?"

"Long. But not long enough." I walk over and give my wife a kiss. "How's the schoolwork coming?" I give Erin's head a rub but she bats my hand away.

"Fine, Dad."

She's been a little distant lately, and I worry for a split second that maybe rumors are circulating at school about me and Brooke Baxter. But I have enough to worry about, so I push that thought from my mind.

It's probably just a phase she's going through. It was so much easier when she was younger. I wonder, again, what it would be like to have a son. Would we relate better to each other? We tried for more kids, but Madeline wasn't able to get pregnant again. It was putting a strain on our marriage, so we both decided to quit while we were ahead rather than resort to fertility treatments.

"When's dinner?" I ask.

"Twenty minutes."

"It smells good."

"Dad. *Shh.* I'm trying to concentrate."

I can't see her face because I'm standing behind her, but I sense there's more to this than an eagerness to do math homework. My eyes meet Madeline's and I shrug. Then she mouths *guy problems.* I nod and decide to take Max for a walk, my one male companion in this female-dominated household. I pat the dog's head rather than disturbing Erin again. Max's hearing isn't what it used to be so I'd have to

almost yell to get his attention. The dog springs up and fol-
lows me to the door.

"Let's go boy."

I relish the eager look on Max's face as I snap on the leash
and head out the door, the only member of the family who'll
continue to look up to me no matter how this mess plays out.

FOUR

Miles

I have to stop myself from laughing out loud at the sheer insanity of the situation I've put myself in. But it wouldn't be a happy laugh. It would be a crazy person laugh. And once I got started, I'd have a hard time stopping. I'd end up in a straightjacket. Considering my other options, that might not be a bad way to go.

Because I've backed myself into an insanely tight corner. And it's likely that nobody would believe me at this point if I came out and told them all the truth. But as I watch Brooke gather up her belongings after our aborted mid-day meet-up, I realize this can't go on for very much longer. It was bad enough when it first started, before I knew what she was really like. But she's grown increasingly more demanding over the last few months, especially after I couldn't deliver the promotion. And now that I think she could have murdered someone, I'm not sure how long I can keep up the ruse.

For a short moment, I consider going to the police. Making a deal with them. Leveling with them, before this gets even more out of control. If she did it, her crime is far worse than the skeletons in my closet. If I could only find some evidence that she had something to do with that teacher's death. But when I attempted to broach the subject a few moments ago, she clammed up, went into the bathroom, and slammed the door. Judging from the pressed lips and tense jawline after she reemerged, she's now livid. And that's not good.

Grabbing my phone, I pretend to check my messages. But I'm actually pulling up a recording app. I keep an eye on her as she slips on her sweater, one arm at a time. The silence is unsettling, but I've decided to be patient. Anything I say will only make it worse.

"Miles," she says finally. She's standing a few feet from me, doing up the bottom buttons of her cardigan.

"What, Brooke?" I press the record button on my phone.

"This isn't working for me." She's not looking at me as she flips her silky chestnut hair out from under her sweater and fluffs it a bit.

"What isn't working for you?"

"This!" She holds out her palms. "We had a deal, and you didn't deliver. And may I remind you that this is a bigger problem for you than it is for me."

"I know that, Brooke."

"So why the hell would you accuse me of killing Kimi Choy?"

"Huh? What are you talking about?"

"I'm not stupid, Miles. I know what you were insinuating with your questions. *Isn't that a strange coincidence? You were just talking about her and now she's dead?*" Brooke says this in a deep, faux man-voice, her nose scrunched and her eyes burning. "Do you think I'm an idiot?"

I'm still holding on to the hope that I can contain this.

"That's not what I—"

"You know what I think, Miles? I think maybe you're a psychopath. Maybe you got that information from me last week, followed her, and pushed her down those stairs. And now you're trying to pin it on me. Maybe you'll do anything to keep your secrets from coming out. And Doug Walker isn't stupid. He's going to figure out what happened soon enough, as soon as they start on the audit. And then you're going down, and you're not taking me with you. I'll blame it all on you. I'll tell them you bullied me into going along with your cover-up. So, I ask you again. Who's got more of a reason to kill Kimi Choy?"

"I didn't kill her, Brooke!"

"*Neither did I!* The police said she fell, so why did you even go there?"

"I didn't 'go there.' I didn't accuse you of anything. You're overreacting."

"I'm not overreacting. You said it was a 'strange coincidence.'"

"It *is* a strange coincidence."

She lets out a sigh, and I pause for a bit.

"Look, I'm sorry you took it that way. I guess I'm starting to get paranoid. You're the only one I can talk to about this, Brooke."

She rolls her eyes.

"What more do you want from me?" I ask.

"Nothing. I want out. I don't want Walker's job anymore, so you can figure out a way to get rid of him that doesn't involve me. This school is a shithole. It's circling the drain, and we both know it. I'm officially on the market. I made the final cut on a head of school job in Denver. I doubt our little scheme would've worked anyway."

I take a deep breath to try and slow my racing heart. If she doesn't want the job, I've lost my leverage. On the other hand, she might just be angry, and that can probably be overcome. She's been mad at me before, and she's gotten over it, with a little cajoling and a lot of patience on my part.

"I'm sorry it's all such a mess. For whatever that's worth," I offer.

"It's worth nothing, Miles."

"I have a plan. I told you. That donor I mentioned? I'm very close to closing the deal with him. Then we won't need the loan. And the audit and all of this mess goes away. Our plan can still work."

"*Your* plan. Not mine. I want out, Miles. I'm done."

"So we just...what? Go our separate ways? Is that what you're saying? Forget about the dirt we planted on Walker? What if it surfaces?"

"If it surfaces, it surfaces. What do I care? People probably won't believe it anyway. The guy's practically a saint. It'll take more than a couple of deep fake videos to change their minds."

"Well, if it works the way we planned, then you'll get the job."

"The way *you* planned, Miles. You're not pinning this on me. And the job in Denver is a better fit for me. It's a day school. I'm sick of living at my job. And I'll be happy to get back to civilization and away from this frozen hell hole. I just told you. I want out."

I feel a squeeze in my chest. I've lost most of my bargaining power if she no longer wants the job, that's true. But she's still complicit in this mess, so I still have something to hold over her.

"Your hands aren't exactly clean here, Brooke, so let's walk carefully through these next few moments."

"Don't threaten me, Miles. Or I'll go to the police and come clean with what I know about you, your company, and your padded invoices. I'll blame it all on you. I'll tell them you bribed me to keep quiet. And that you threatened me. And then everyone will know you've been pilfering the school for the last few years. You've got a lot more to lose than I do, and don't you forget it."

Brooke turns on her heels and heads for the door, and I shut off the recording app on my phone. I hope she's bluffing and that I can calm her down later. But just in case, I have something on her. I've got her admitting she planted dirt on Doug Walker, and I have her on blackmail. I can edit out the unflattering parts later to suit my purposes.

But I'm not going to spring that on her now. We don't speak again as she grabs her purse and heads out the door, leaving me alone with my thoughts.

How did things get so out of control?

It had all started pretty innocently. I was finishing up an office suite project in Albany when the pandemic hit, and I did what I had to do to keep my business afloat. Companies abandoned their buildings for remote work, making the project practically worthless. I was about to lose everything, including my good name and my credit, if I didn't make my bridge loan payment.

And then an opportunity presented itself. The school needed a new student center and an additional student dormitory. We decided to go full steam ahead with both projects, taking advantage of the dwindling student body, which made the construction much easier. I won the bid, which wasn't hard because the two competitor bids were fake and even higher than mine. Nobody paid much attention at the time; we had bigger worries.

It became a cash cow—the school paid in full whatever invoices I sent. An arrangement I had with former Head of School Butch McDonnell, who was happy to take his share. Then Brooke started to ask questions, and I eventually had to cut her in on the deal, too. I would have made things right eventually by doing the next project at cost—a new faculty housing center to replace the rickety structure on the opposite side of campus. But as the pandemic raged on and the school lost more than half of its tuition revenue, the board delayed that project and started to tighten belts.

As the school's financial situation grew more dire, the board started prying into the finances. My buddy Butch MacDonald bailed, taking early retirement, and washing his hands of the situation. And I tried to install Brooke in his place to buy some time to figure out how to make this all go away. A plan that's now blowing up in my face.

Because Doug Walker got the job instead, and he's now trying to convince the board to take a loan to tide the school over rather than freeze wages or cut services or hike tuition to stay afloat. If the school goes through with the loan, it will trigger an independent audit. And that will most certainly expose what I did.

I have a plan to fix it, but I need more time. Just a little more time to win over this new big money donor and make it all go away. That's one reason they need me—I bring in donor money. Even with what I diverted to cover the bridge loan, the school is way ahead of the game because of my tenure on the board. Hopefully that will make a difference if the scandal breaks.

What I did is unethical, for sure. It would shame me if it came out, and by extension, my family. The school would probably sue me and I might get prosecuted and fined. I don't think it's something that would land me in prison, although I should probably check with my attorney on that.

But with the death of this teacher, it's all changed. Sure, it could have been an accident. But my imagination is running wild with *what-ifs*.

What if Brooke killed her?

What if she didn't do it, but she thinks I did?

What if she's so angry, she tries to frame me?

My mind is spinning, and there's nobody I can talk to about it. I should have gone to Madeline back when it all started falling apart. But I couldn't bring myself to burst her bubble. I couldn't bear to disappoint her. So here I am, on the verge of total collapse. And the one person who might be able to comfort me and help figure a way out is off limits.

But I'm not going down without a fight. With a quick computer search, I locate the only school in Denver that has a head of school opening. I send off an email to the consultant heading up the search. The issue of Brooke's caustic management style will likely come up anyway when they do their deep background, but I'm not taking any chances. If this is how she wants to play it, I'll use all the resources at my disposal to cut her off at the knees.

She can't leave now. Our little scheme can still work. It *will* work. We'll get rid of Doug Walker. Brooke will take the job. I'll close the deal with the donor. And we'll fix it.

FIVE

Cassie

Maybe I'm going crazy. It's possible. Anyone could go stir-crazy up here on this frozen mountain.

It's been two days since I sent the email to the facilities team. As expected, nobody cut back the tree branches. The scraping at my window at night is driving me mad, and I'm not getting enough sleep. Under normal circumstances, I would consider using earplugs. But I don't like the idea of not being able to hear someone outside my apartment.

This isn't an irrational fear. I have a legitimate reason to be afraid all the time, even without Kimi's untimely and suspicious death. But now it's even worse. I also have the distinct feeling the administration isn't telling us everything. And the other day, I could swear a dark green SUV was following me as I did my errands in town. It wouldn't be the first time I've been followed.

It seems almost impossible to me that Kimi fell down the stairs with enough velocity to actually die from her injuries. I think something's up and they just don't want to cause a panic.

So, who could have done it?

Well, for starters, there are a few terrifying students at this school I wouldn't want to meet in a dark alley. As I said, they're scraping the bottom of the barrel here as far as filling seats. And in the current academic climate, anyone who isn't an easy grader is a target of student wrath. Grade inflation these days is totally insane, but I try to hold the line, as did Kimi. I think about that scandal a few years back when parents broke the law and went to prison trying to sidestep the system to get their kids into their preferred colleges. How far would the shadier ones go to get rid of a tough grader? I don't want to find out.

Then there's Dan, the miracle teacher. Hunks can be murderers too. Just this morning, I saw him huddled in the hallway with Brooke Baxter, speaking in hushed tones. Brooke was facing me, so I couldn't see Dan's face, but it looked a bit intimate for two people who'd just met. When I approached them, she caught my eye, pulled back a little, and stopped talking. Looking back, I suppose the closeness could have been a mild flirtation. But there was something about her furrowed brow that made me feel it was something more clandestine. And it made me question his sudden appearance out of nowhere.

Is he really an English teacher? Or is he a plant, in cahoots with Brooke to take over the school and eliminate anyone who stands in her way? Is that why she put Dan next to me? Because she thinks I was friends with Kimi and she might have told me something?

Or was it one of the many faculty members who had it in for Kimi? Did one of them take it upon themselves to silence her? I have a hard time believing one of them would actually push her down the stairs, but then you never know. We could have a homicidal psychopath in our midst. Of course, there's always the possibility it was a psychotic stranger. Random violence has escalated in the last couple of years, at least in the city. Maybe it's made its way upstate.

And the more I mull all of it over, an accident really does seem the least likely explanation, and I wonder why the police aren't investigating further. Suffice to say, I won't be using earplugs to muffle the tree branches anytime soon. I made good on my promise to send a copy of Kimi's letter to the police. And although I was careful, I'm concerned they will somehow trace it back to me.

"Time!" I call out. "Put down your pens and stop writing."

I'm one of the few teachers who still gives in-class essays. At least I'm giving it on a Wednesday, not a Monday, morning. The chatting begins as I start to walk around and pick up their exams, and I immediately miss the silence. There's nothing like the energy I feel when I watch my students hard at work on their exams. The room positively hums with all that focused concentration. It feels a bit like being thrown into a cold pool of water when the ruckus returns.

As I finish making my way around the room, I see Erin Kensington, a promising senior and one of my strongest students, with her head in her hands.

"Erin? Are you okay?"

She doesn't answer me. "Can I go to the bathroom?" she asks instead.

"Of course." We only have a few minutes of class left, but something seems terribly wrong so I let her leave. She takes her things with her. Then the rest of the students get restless and start to pack up.

"You can go a few minutes early," I say.

They leave, and I start paging through the exams. I pull out Erin's because I like to start with the better essays, and I'm troubled but not surprised to see that she's written very little, for her. She was obviously upset about something this morning. After I read through all of them and get a better handle on her performance, I'll reach out to her and maybe to the family to see if there's anything going on. She's a day student and the daughter of the school board chair. A minor real estate mogul named Miles Kensington.

But that's not why I'm going the extra mile. I'd do it for any of my students, although I'll keep it in mind that her father's the board chair when I draft my email. You never know how a family like hers will take it if I express my concerns. In the meantime, I'm going to be late for my first meeting as department chair.

Only two more weeks until winter break. I can make it.

"I have to do *what?*" I feel my eyes widen and my nostrils flare, and I actually think about quitting. Just plain storming out. But I can't. I had hardly any savings when Evan dumped me and I started this job. The one and only benefit to being stranded here, living rent free, is that I have nothing to spend money on. I've saved quite a bit so far but not nearly enough.

If I quit, my only option would be to move in with my parents, and that's not a viable one for me. I wasn't even planning to go see them for Christmas. But I've already booked a trip to Florida to see an old college friend. And now they want me to stay here for most of the break on a skeleton crew that will watch over a handful of students who have nowhere to go.

Are they insane?

"Why me?" I ask Brooke.

But I already know the answer.

I'm single. I don't have a family. I don't have a sickly mother like Judy Prather. Or little children who have their hearts set on going to Disney World like the social studies department chair. And I'm new. I have no seniority. She informs me that she and the head of school will also be in residence most of the time, but they will technically be off duty.

"I've offered to stay too," my buddy Ed says, which provides some measure of comfort. He does have seniority, so he doesn't need to do this. I have a feeling he might be doing it just to keep me company. That, and with his wife gone, he probably doesn't feel like celebrating the holidays anyway, which is heartbreaking. I'm thankful that at least I'll have him here with me.

Brooke offers to try to work out a way to let me go to Florida for a few days, but I tell them it's not worth it. By the time I pay for transportation to the airport and the cost of airfare, it's too much of an expense for a few days of warmth. I'll move the ticket to spring break. The only reason I was even going is that I had a free place to stay and I'm going stir-crazy here. Maybe I can strike a deal for them to turn up the heat as my Christmas bonus.

I think about the fact that it will feel even more deserted here over break than it does now. On the one hand, fewer people means there's less chance that the murderer will be here with me. On the other hand, fewer people means the chance of my survival goes down if the murderer stays over break.

The murderer.

I've already convinced myself there's a campus murderer on the loose, and I have to admit, the mystery lover in me is a bit intrigued. I've been addicted to mystery novels since I was young, and I can't help but play the various scenarios over and over in my head about what may have happened to Kimi. Plus, I can't stop thinking about the letter she sent me. And it's killing me that I'll probably never know what became of it after I sent it to the police.

If I'm being honest, I'm not too worried about my own safety. If Kimi was murdered, why would the person be after me? It makes no sense. Nobody here knows that she sent me a letter. It's just my nature to be proactive, to be prepared for every possible threat that might come my way. I decide I'll start carrying my pepper spray with me from now on though, just in case. If anyone here is thinking about pushing me down the stairs, they better think again.

"So, it's me and Ed and that's it?"

"Oh, and Dan Moralis. He's staying too," Brooke replies.

So, Dan will be right next door to me on a deserted high school campus over a long and frigid two-week holiday break. My imagination runs wild as I picture us colliding in the hallway again. But I can't decide if it's the beginning of a steamy romance novel or the opening scene of a slasher movie.

SIX

Cassie

It's Monday morning, the week before winter break, and I'm not even excited. I've finished grading the last essay exams, calculating the final semester grades, and writing comments for the report cards. After hours of tedious work, I'm finished, and about to head out to lunch. This usually puts me in a fabulous mood. But now that I'll be stuck here over break, it feels anticlimactic. I wonder how I'll ever pass the time without my classes to distract me.

I'm hoping to get into the city at least once or twice if the weather permits, but it's not easy to get there. We're on the opposite side of the Hudson River from the train line. To get to the city, I have to drive down the icy, snowy mountain, cross a rickety, narrow bridge over to the Poughkeepsie train station, then take a two-hour-long train ride to Grand Central.

I'd love to go see a Broadway show, but they are so expensive. That's the trouble with Manhattan. It's the greatest city in the world…if you have money. At least in San Diego I could walk on the beach or hike or do something that doesn't cost a fortune. I could try the day-of discount ticket booth, but it's all dependent on the weather. I'm terrified to drive in snow and ice, being from California, so I'll have to play it by ear. It will be a miracle if I don't go stir-crazy over the next two weeks.

I start to put in the final semester grades. As I expected, Erin Kensington's essay was subpar. She's one of my best writers, but her final essay was about a C, although I'll upgrade that to the gentleman's B minus. Most of the others were about what I expected. One lower grade didn't bring her average down all that much. I weigh the pros and cons of getting myself any further involved. I did email her to ask if something was wrong, but all I got back was a single line. **Thanks. I'm fine**.

I could leave it at that, but then I remember the troubled look on her face and decide I'll say something to the family. Most parents would take it the right way, and I'm truly concerned about her. I'll contact her mother though, not the board chair. I know she heads up the parent group for the senior class and does some volunteering here, although we've never met. I go back and forth about how to word the email, and then I fire it off, close my laptop, and head over to lunch.

───────

"Hey, Ed," I say as I get in line with my tray and consider the dining options. When I first arrived here, it seemed like there was a lot to choose from. But after nearly a semester, I'm tired of the offerings: salad and sandwich bar, a hot option with meat and without. I have a kitchenette in my room with a small fridge, stove-top, and microwave, but no oven. I could cook for myself, I suppose, but I feel like it's a waste of money to buy food when free meals are part of my compensation.

"Hey, Cass." He pats me on the back. "Sorry you got the short end of the stick."

I opt for some salad and a roll, while Ed fills his plate with a rubbery-looking chicken dish that looks risky to me.

"It's fine. I'm the new girl."

"Let's go into the city one day over break," he says. "I can drive us."

"I'd love that."

I smile at the thought of being driven to the city rather than having to make that awful trek by myself. Ed knows I'm really upset about having to stay over break, and he's trying so hard to make it tolerable for me here. He's lived this boarding school lifestyle for an eternity, and I pause to consider whether he might be taking my unhappiness personally like it's some sort of criticism of him. Until this year, he'd always been here with his wife. I think about whether it would be more tolerable with a partner. Maybe, but it's still not for me.

"Ms. Romano?" A student of mine, a tenth grader named Marko from Ukraine, walks up to me as we're heading to a table. "Can I meet with you during office hours today about my essay?"

I smile at him. "Sure, Marko. I'll be there."

He didn't really need to ask me. And he probably doesn't need help with his essay. He's a very strong writer, better than many of my native English speakers. And he knows he can come anytime to my office hours. That's why they're called office hours.

But he's one of those kids who hangs around teachers a lot. He comes early to class and waits outside the door for the other students to leave so he can come in and take a seat as soon as possible, even before class starts. I can tell he's lonely and scared. His parents sent him here to get away from the war, but they're back in Ukraine. I'm sure he's terrified for them.

We don't have many European boarders here, most are from Asia or the U.S., and places like this can get a little cliquish. Kimi told me that her old school had a buddy system of sorts, where they paired the local day kids with a boarding student to help them adjust. We talked about starting that here, but then it dropped off the radar. I think I'll bring it up at the next administrative meeting, and I'll give Kimi the credit for suggesting it.

As Ed and I are getting settled at a table, I glance around to see if I can spot Dan, which is pretty much the only entertainment I have these days. I feel like I'm in high school again, darting my eyes around the room to see if I can spot my crush. For a guy who lives next door to me, I don't run into him much.

I did have a short meeting with him and the rest of my department, and it went well. Very professional. I'm getting better at warding off his effect on me. At least on the surface. But then I haven't been alone with him since that first time in the hall outside of our apartments.

"How're the final grades shaping up?" Ed asks.

I give him the rundown. We teach some of the same students for one of our courses, so we sometimes compare notes about students. I mention Erin Kensington and her subpar essay. Although he doesn't have her this semester, he remembers her as one of his strongest the year before. Then he bites his lip and looks off to the side.

"Ed. What is it?" I ask.

"It's probably nothing."

"What's probably nothing?"

His jaw tenses a bit. "I don't like to gossip."

"I'm not asking you to gossip. I'm just asking if you can help me figure out what's wrong with my student."

He looks off to the side as he taps his fingers on the table top. Then he turns back to me.

"Her father's the board chair. Miles Kensington," he says.

"Yes, I know that."

"And he backed Brooke for the head of school job. Over Doug."

"Okay. And?"

"And there were some people who speculated that he had ulterior motives for backing Brooke."

"Like?" Now I'm the one tapping my fingers on the table top. I wish he'd just spit it out.

"Like maybe they were 'involved.'" His fingers fly up into air quotes.

I think about the fact that I emailed Erin's mother, and my stomach lurches. That could have been a big mistake if that's what Erin's upset about.

What if she knows, and I'm rubbing salt in the wound?

I tell my fears to Ed, and he goes on to ease my worries. He assures me that Madeline's really nice and down-to-earth, and that she'll probably appreciate the heads-up. All the teachers like her. She was an educator for a while, and she's really supportive of faculty.

"Speak of the devil," he says.

"What?"

"That's her. Right over there."

He points to a tall, slim, striking woman with reddish-brown hair cascading down her back. She reminds me of the Little Mermaid. She turns towards us, and I get a better look at her face. She must be at least mid-forties with a daughter as old as Erin, but she doesn't look it.

She has a girl-next-door kind of beauty that ages well. She's dressed down, wearing jeans and a sweater, smiling and making the rounds. And I breathe a sigh of relief. As a former teacher, she'll likely appreciate the fact that I contacted her.

She looks vaguely familiar to me, but I can't place her. I've probably seen her around school if she's here as much as

Ed says. Or maybe I've seen her around town. There aren't many places to go, so it's possible I've seen her at the supermarket or the coffee shop.

"Personally, I don't believe it." He shakes his head.

"You don't believe what?" I say.

"That Brooke's sleeping with the board chair. He did go to bat for her on the head of school job. But that doesn't mean anything. And it's so typical, accusing a woman of sleeping with someone to get ahead. But you know how people are. Even if it's not true, it could be bothering Erin if she caught wind of it."

"You think the students heard it?"

"I'm not sure." He presses his lips. "I don't think something at the board level would be on their radar, but you never know. They're more apt to speculate about teachers. They saw Judy and me downtown together one Saturday getting coffee a few years ago, and that was all it took for rumors to start flying. And I was married at the time. We just laughed it off. They're bored. It happens."

I take this as a cautionary tale and remind myself to stay cool and professional with Dan. I don't need rumors floating around about me.

"But you don't believe it?"

"Look, Brooke's got a caustic bedside manner. It's true. But she's efficient and smart, which is a lot more than I can say about our former head of school. His golf score was more important to him than our SAT scores. And he made some terrible financial decisions. Nearly ran the school into the ground. She wasn't a horrible choice. She's ambitious, sure. But I expect she'd get a lot less flack for it if she were a man."

"Wow, Ed, you're quite the feminist." I smile.

"You can thank Susie for that." He lets out a sigh, and I see the sadness fill his eyes again. Susie's his late wife, and I remind myself that this is his first Christmas alone. He doesn't have children and his parents have passed, but I'm surprised he doesn't have other family members or friends who can help him through this.

"You must miss her. Especially this time of year."

"I wouldn't wish this on anyone."

"Do you have any family close by? I can cover things here if you want to get away for a bit." I pick at my salad. I tried a new dressing to get some variety, and it's much spicier than I anticipated. It's not sitting well with me.

"Nobody I care to spend time with. At least not right now. Susie was pretty much my world."

I understand exactly what he means. Maybe we're a good pair, Ed and me. Two Christmas misfits stranded on a frozen mountain. Waiting to see if a murderer strikes again.

"What about you? Don't your parents want to see you?"

I hate this question, although I'm the one who started talking about our families.

Me and my big mouth.

"Um, yeah, I'm sure they do. But they understand that I have to stay."

"You should tell them to come visit. You could show them around the city," Ed says.

"They hate the cold," I offer, hoping to move away from this topic. "But we need to figure out some ways to pass the time. Any ideas?"

Ed takes a bite of his rubber chicken and shrugs.

I know I shouldn't be so hard on my parents. They're not horrible people or anything. And although they have their flaws, I suppose it's a comfort to know they're still around. I probably shouldn't take that for granted. But I have my reasons for distancing myself from them, reasons I don't want to dwell on right now.

Suddenly, a loud crash reverberates through the dining commons.

"Oh my God," someone yells out.

Our heads whip around to see Doug Walker, our head of school, with his hand on a table, trying to steady himself. His tray and its contents are splattered all over the floor. He's clutching his chest and taking deep breaths, and we're all frozen to our chairs.

Shouldn't someone be doing something?

Brooke Baxter runs over from the other side of the room and takes him by the arm. She pulls out a chair for him. "Doug. Have a seat," we hear her say.

"I'm okay," he says. But he sits down anyway.

"It's okay, everyone," Brooke calls out with a wave of her hand, indicating that we should all mind our own business, but everyone remains fixated on them for a bit longer as she takes the seat next to him.

They're talking softly now, so we can't hear them, but Walker's facing us, and after a bit, I see him smile. That's a good sign. The last thing we need is another dead body a week before winter break. One death I can look past. *But two?* That might be enough to send me back to my parents' house, despite my misgivings.

"He has a heart condition," Ed says to me.

"I heard that. But why do people even know about it? It seems kind of personal."

Ed goes on to tell me that the issue of Walker's prior heart attack came up during the interview process. Apparently, one of the parents on the interview panel knew about it and grilled him about his fitness for the job. That seems a bit over the top to me. Would a parent really take it upon themselves to dig up that information and then question a candidate about it?

I think about Kimi's letter, and I wonder if someone— like Brooke Baxter—could have put someone onto it. How far would she have gone to get the job? Then I quickly wipe that thought from my mind.

Don't engage. Do your time. Move on.

One of the maintenance guys—a fifty-something long-timer named Tommy—is cleaning up the mess. Walker stands up from his chair, looks down at the floor, and starts to bend down like he might try to help. But then he straightens up and places his hand on the table as if he's dizzy. After a few moments, he smiles, gives everyone a wave, and goes on his way.

I don't believe in coincidences, so now I can't stop thinking about Kimi's letter and her warning that Baxter was plotting something against Doug Walker. I'm starting to wish I hadn't sent it to the police anonymously, because I need to keep my concerns to myself. If I hadn't sent it, perhaps I could come forward now and voice them.

I haven't said anything to anyone about packing up Kimi's room. I think I'll just go do it and not ask permission. We gave each other spare keys months ago, so I can go in anytime I want. Maybe there's something in her room that will give me more of a clue about what's going on. Packing up will give me an excuse to snoop around a bit if someone questions me.

So much for staying out of it.

The one saving grace is that all this sleuthing will give me something to do to keep me from dying of boredom over break. I try to convince myself that I have no reason to think her death was anything more than a tragic accident. In all likelihood, there's no killer here.

I tell myself that this will be fun. A distraction. Me and my vivid imagination, stuck on top of a frozen mountain, playing detective for two weeks.

And that's my best-case scenario.

SEVEN

Miles

When I come through the front door, Madeline's seated on our living room sofa sipping something from a coffee mug, but it's too late in the day for caffeine. Probably herbal tea.

"Did you hear about Doug Walker?" she asks.

It's Tuesday afternoon, and I've just returned from two nights away in Albany. A business trip for a residential development project I'm bidding on that will, hopefully, pull us out of our financial quagmire. I'm getting ready to go upstairs to our bedroom, but I stop and turn to my wife.

"What about him?" I ask.

The time away did me some good. But with that one sentence, the sinking feeling has returned. Maybe the videos have surfaced and the smear campaign is in motion? But I'm sure I would have heard about that.

"He had some kind of heart episode. At lunch. In front of everyone," she says.

"Oh wow." I had not heard about it. And for that reason, I assume it was nothing major. But I'm a bit surprised that

Brooke didn't contact me to tell me about it. Maybe she really is set on moving on, leaving this place behind.

"I was there. I saw the whole thing."

Madeline goes on to tell me how Walker dropped his tray of food in the cafeteria in front of a room full of people and then had to steady himself to keep from keeling over. Then she tells me that Brooke Baxter came to Walker's rescue, likely scoring some PR points in the process.

"That came up when we were doing the head of school search. His heart issue," I say.

"I remember."

Madeline volunteers at the school and serves on committees, that sort of thing. But she could probably be running the place if she'd stayed in the workforce. She was a principal at an elementary school years ago—quite an accomplishment at thirty-two—but she decided to give up her career and be a stay-at-home mom for a while after Erin was born. I always thought she'd go back into education when Erin got older. But she didn't, and I never pressed the issue, although I've hinted at it.

I thought about leveling with her a few years ago when we were in financial trouble. Asking her to go back to work and pitch in. But I just couldn't. My wife grew up dirt poor, unlike me. She's worked her whole life, even as a teenager. Marrying me was supposed to be the end of a life plagued by financial pressures. I couldn't bring myself to lay my troubles at her feet.

"Is he okay?" I ask, trying not to think about the fact that if he isn't, it could bode well for me and my troubles.

Madeline shrugs. "I suppose. I haven't heard any more about it."

When she heads off to the kitchen I start upstairs with my suitcase. I need to see Brooke and find out what's going on, but we've been in a bit of a standoff. I've seen her only once, at Falcon Ridge, since she lashed out at me in the motel room. Based on that one time, I sense she might be calming down a bit. She even joked around with me at the meeting. But then, that meeting was at school, and there were other people around.

Still, I caught her eye for a moment, and she smiled, like maybe she was warming back up to me. Perhaps the news that she wasn't moving on in the Denver head of school search changed her attitude. On the other hand, it could have been a smile of delight as she relished the thought of screwing me to the wall.

I'm not in the mood to talk to her now, so I fire off a text and ask if we can meet for coffee in the morning, which seems a reasonably neutral course of action. With that taken care of, I'm comforted by the prospect of a quiet dinner at home with my wife.

As I'm unpacking, I'm struggling to recall my conversation with Brooke, the one that got her concerned that Kimi Choy was onto us. Because if Kimi Choy suspected something, it's quite possible the teacher's suspicions didn't die with her. It's a tight community up on that hill, so she could have mentioned it to someone, in the event Kimi really did overhear what Brooke thinks she overheard.

It was two days before the teacher's death. I was on my burner and Brooke was at school, on her cell. In all probability, only one side of the conversation would have been audible. But you never know with cell phones. It didn't sound like she had me on speaker, although I'm pretty sure she said my name at least once. As I play the conversation over in my head, I'm comforted by the recollection that Brooke's voice wasn't that loud, maybe a hair above a whisper.

I tried talking him out of the loan, Miles. He's not budging, Brooke said.

The plan was to have her try to talk Doug Walker out of the loan by convincing him that putting the school into debt would be a terrible legacy. A bad way to start his tenure. And by offering to find places to cut spending instead.

Did you try the legacy angle? I'd asked.

Of course! He's not having it. He wants to be liked, not feared. Nobody likes a guy who comes in and puts benefits and professional development funds on the chopping block. You better hope the scandal breaks soon, or we're screwed. It's all going to come out.

I'm very close on the donor. We need to stall him. We need time.

We don't have time! He needs to go. Soon. Or you need to fix this. I'm not going down for this. We need a plan—

Brooke had stopped, abruptly, to address someone—Kimi Choy, it turned out—who'd entered the room.

Do you need something?

At the time, I was the one who was concerned. But Brooke assured me there was nothing to worry about. She pointed out that she'd been speaking softly. And that the teacher only heard the tail end of the conversation.

But there's something titillating about a whisper. It makes people strain to listen even harder. And Kimi Choy could have been standing there a while before she was seen. Still, Brooke was there and I wasn't, so I deferred to her and let it go.

Until a few days later, that Friday afternoon, when Brooke called me in a panic, informing me that Kimi Choy left a resignation letter in her mailbox that afternoon, saying something about a family emergency in North Carolina. But Brooke wasn't buying it. She started to freak out.

Do you think she heard us the other day? What if she's planning to turn us in?

At the time, I thought the best course of action was to do nothing and let the woman leave town. And Brooke eventually came around.

Turn us in for what? I said. *We haven't done anything she could possibly know about. Calm down. It'll be fine.*

But then the next morning Kimi Choy was found dead at the Cortlandt train station. Thankfully, Brooke was smart enough to shred the resignation letter and keep her mouth shut, so nobody else knows the Choy woman was planning to quit her job and leave town. At least I hope nobody else knows, because that wouldn't be good.

But it's been a while and nobody's come forward. And I tell myself I'm probably in the clear. If the police suspected her death was something other than an accident, they'd likely have acted on it by now.

As I'm putting away my toiletries, I catch a glimpse of myself in the bathroom mirror. It seems like my gray hairs have mushroomed over the last few weeks, and my "rugged good looks" have turned ragged: dark circles under my eyes, a sallow undertone to my ruddy complexion. The stress is getting to me, and I wonder if it shows to anyone besides me.

I slap some water on my face, take a deep breath, and force my face into a smile. That seems to help a bit, making me look less severe. I'll keep that in mind when I go downstairs.

———

"I got an email from Erin's English teacher," Madeline says.

The two of us have just sat down to dinner, and my wife is catching me up on everything. Erin stayed late at school to rehearse for the Christmas concert and will be driven home by another parent, so we're enjoying some much-needed alone time. I have an awkwardly large mouthful of filet mignon so I can't reply immediately, but I'm guessing that it isn't good news.

I hold up a finger, swallow, and take a sip of water. "What kind of email?"

"She said Erin's last essay exam wasn't up to par. And that she was visibly upset about something in class the other day. It didn't affect her semester grade. The teacher was more concerned about her emotional state."

"Didn't you say something about guy problems?"

Madeline nods as she chews and swallows her food, then takes a sip of her white wine. "I'm not sure that's the reason though."

"Was she seeing someone?"

"No. But she liked a guy in her drama class, and he asked out her friend. I think she was a little disappointed, but I don't see that affecting her schoolwork."

"Then what do you think it is?"

"I have no idea. Maybe it's nothing. Or maybe it's something else. She doesn't tell me everything, Miles."

"Should I talk to her?"

"No. Don't worry about it. I've got this. I'm just trying to keep you in the loop."

The guilt hits me hard, right in the gut.

If Erin's upset now, how will she feel if a scandal breaks and I'm hauled off to prison?

But I nod my head and force myself to smile. Then I change the subject and start to fill my wife in on my latest project, a midsize condo development that could really turn things around for us. If I can just keep the school situation from blowing up in my face, this deal might be the answer to our money problems.

"It sounds promising," she says, and we continue to eat in comfortable silence.

As I munch on an asparagus stalk, I think about Walker's heart condition and the fact that if something unfortunate were to incapacitate him, Brooke could be promoted to interim head of school and stave off the audit until I can close the donation. I realize that's a terrible thought to have about a nice guy, but I'm desperate.

After we're done eating, we clear the dishes together and start to rinse and stack them in the dishwasher. I'm suddenly struck with an overwhelming desire to make love to my wife. I come up behind her and run my hands up the sides of her taut, thin frame. I lift her hair and kiss her softly on the back of the neck. She arches her back, and I feel her body respond, usually a good sign.

Then I whisper in her ear, "We've got the house to ourselves. How 'bout a spin on the couch?"

She rubs back against me but then lets out a deep sigh. "Not tonight. Bad timing." Then she turns around to face me and places her hand on my arm. "I'll make it up to you this weekend. Erin's staying with her friend Saturday night."

"Is that a promise?"

"That's a promise."

We share an intimate kiss and I sneak in a butt squeeze. It will have to be enough for now.

"You drive me crazy," I say.

"I know." Madeline smiles.

As I scrub the pans and my wife wipes the counters, an idea starts to form in my mind. If Doug Walker's health issue is serious enough, maybe I could offer the man a short-term medical leave. That would give me the space to figure a way out, and I'd also come out looking like a good guy.

Not a bad idea.

Except for Brooke, the wild card. If Walker's departure would allow her to step up as interim head of school, that might be enough to get her under control. I need to see her and take her temperature.

Soon.

A few minutes later, I feel my phone vibrate. Drying off my hands, I reach into my pocket to check it. It's a text from Brooke, confirming our meeting tomorrow.

And she ended it with a smiley face.

EIGHT

Cassie

Kimi's apartment is only one floor below me, and I have yet to enter her room. It's Wednesday, and I have her spare key. But I haven't been able to bring myself to walk down and open the door. I will make myself do it, though. Tonight. Before any potential evidence is gone forever.

It's not that I'm afraid of running into a murderer. And it's not because I'm avoiding the inevitable emotional wave that will surely hit me when I start looking through her things. It's the anticipation of walking into her apartment and seeing her life there, all neat and tidy, waiting for her to return, but knowing that she never will. This nearly paralyzes me.

I was thirteen years old when my entire world was turned upside down. It was just after dinner, and I still can't bring myself to eat chicken marsala. That's what we had for dinner that night, and the shocking news made me sick to my stomach. So sick that, to this day, the smell of that dish brings me right back to that moment with all of its emotional punch. I avoid chicken marsala like the plague.

It had been a great day up until that point because in math class, Tad, this boy I liked, finally smiled at me. I had a tingly feeling for the rest of the day, and my step felt lighter as I bounced around from class to class. My senses were heightened with anticipation as I fantasized about our first kiss. I imagined it would start out gentle and then get steamier, like in the movies. He had a bit of an edge to him, but he was no slacker. He was smart and seemed a bit older than his years. I heard he even hung out with high school kids sometimes.

I'd had a crush on Tad for months, and I'd been making some progress. I'd been getting in more with the popular girls, something that had taken a year or so of effort, and that seemed to be upping my social status. It was a long-term strategy. And it was working. I was thinking about him as we were finishing up dinner, when my mother turned to me and uttered the words that would change my life.

We need to have a talk, Cassie.

At first, I thought I was in trouble. When I slept over at a new friend's house the weekend before, her parents were out most of the evening. So she took some of their vodka, mixed it with orange juice, and suggested we have a little fun. I didn't really want to drink it. But I was afraid of looking like a dork. I only had a few sips, pretending to go along with it. But I was convinced my mother knew about it. I almost came right out and confessed, but then I thought better of it.

"Am I in trouble?" I asked.

"No, honey. Not at all." Mom shot my father a menacing look, and he hung his head, averting her death glare. "You've done nothing wrong."

This was uncharted territory. My father was a gregarious man, happy-go-lucky. The life of the party. I'd never seen him so somber. And the glare my mother gave him? I'd never seen her look at him like that before. I assumed right away they were splitting up. Whatever it was, it was clearly his fault. I figured it was an affair, like what had happened to my friend Samantha the year before. Now she had to divide her time between two homes, one of which also housed her father's new girlfriend. The thought of that put my stomach in knots.

"Are you getting a divorce?"

"No," she said. "Look, Cassie, I'm not going to lie to you. We are in a dangerous situation, and you're going to need to listen carefully and do everything we tell you. This is serious. Do you understand?"

I felt a pounding in my chest.

Dangerous? What is she talking about?

It's all sort of a blur when I think back on it. I remember my mother doing most of the talking. We were moving, she said. Leaving town. Changing our names. Leaving our lives behind. I struggled to process what was happening.

What about Tad? What about my friends?

I tried to shake myself awake, figuring it was some sort of bad dream. Maybe some movie I'd seen was stuck in my head, and I was trapped in it. But she just kept on going. Something about my dad being a witness. Police protection. Rules I had to follow. But it wasn't making any sense.

"Are you all going crazy? I can't leave!"

I stood up, pressed my hands against my head, and started pacing around the dining room. My heart raced and a wave of nausea hit me. I kept hoping it was all a nightmare or some kind of misunderstanding. But my mom just kept on going. About witness protection. My dad doing something illegal. Something about my dad being stupid.

"I'm so sorry, honey," I heard him say, but it just pissed me off more.

Wasn't I the teenager? Wasn't I the one who was supposed to do stupid things?

Mom kept talking and talking, but the words weren't making any sense to me. I felt like I was underwater, hearing only the muffled remnants of her words. She talked until I couldn't take it anymore.

"Stop. Mom. Just stop!" My hands flew up into the air as my shrill demand echoed through the house. I needed her to stop talking so I could process what she was saying.

And she did. Finally.

We were all silent for a bit, and everything came to a standstill. I couldn't even look at my parents, but I could see in my periphery they were frozen to their seats. Then my body was racked with sobs as the reality of the situation hit me.

My parents are serious. This isn't a dream.

It felt like my gut was turning inside out, and I thought I might throw up. I stumbled to the living room and collapsed on the sofa as my mother's words reverberated in my brain.

Witness. Illegal. New identity.

And finally, I let myself land on the one word that made me grow up on the spot, the word that shattered my innocence and robbed me of my childhood forever.

Dangerous.

———

I enter Kimi's room and start to look around, and I have to laugh at the irony of the situation. Growing up the way I did, I intentionally picked the most low-key, innocuous profession I could possibly think of. One where I could keep a low profile. One devoid of danger, publicity, or intrigue. I've always loved to read, which is understandable. With no siblings and the fact that I had to keep friends at a distance from middle school on, I lost myself in books. My career choice was between English teacher and librarian. I don't like to sit still, so I landed on teacher. And here I am now, an English teacher intentionally embroiling myself in a possible murder investigation.

I don't see Kimi's computer or any electronics, and I wonder if she took her school computer with her or if they've already taken it. I was hoping to see if I could get into her device and look at her files.

I head into the bedroom and poke around a bit in her closet. Most of her clothes are still hanging there, and I wonder for the millionth time what the feds did with the clothes I left behind when we fled that next morning. Did they donate them or just dump them in the trash? I never asked because it seemed like such a stupid question.

I walk over to her desk. The surface is clean and tidy. There's a marked-up copy of *Adventures of Huckleberry Finn* and a blank notepad. That's it. Either she took everything with her, or somebody already came in and got her teaching materials. I open the drawers, and they're all empty except for a few stray rubber bands and paper clips.

I don't think I'm going to glean anything major from the contents of this apartment, but I go check the bathroom just in case. Shampoo, conditioner, and body wash bottles still sit in the shower caddy. Her medicine cabinet contains contact lens solution, makeup, hair ties, and over-the-counter medications. I notice some prescription eye drops and check the date. The drops are from last August, so if she was leaving town, she probably wouldn't have needed to take them with her.

Judging from what she left behind, it's hard to tell if she planned to come back or if she was outright fleeing. I would think she'd have taken more of her things if she was not planning to come back at all, so I'm leaning more towards the idea that she was coming back. But then again, the desk is suspiciously barren, and she did send me that letter. There are also no important documents that I can see. No passport. No birth certificate. She must have taken all that with her.

I'm snapped out of my musings by the sound of the apartment door creaking open. I freeze for a moment and then reach for my pepper spray. I've been looking over my shoulder since I was thirteen, and even if nothing untoward happened to Kimi, someone could always be after me.

I'd like to think that what happened between my father and his associates was so long ago they've lost interest in him. But I don't take any chances. And we're still technically under federal protection, so there must be some ongoing cause for concern.

Someone is in the room now, and I think about calling out to them. I don't. Instead, I stay hidden in the bathroom. Anyone nosing around will probably come in here eventually. But I have the element of surprise on my side, and I decide it's better to keep it that way.

I hear the desk drawers open and close. Then I hear the person stop, as if they may have heard me in here. I flatten myself against the wall far enough away from the door so I can see them in the mirror but they can't see me. Then I put my thumb on the pepper spray button and get ready to depress it.

I hear footsteps, and I don't dare move a muscle. Then I see him in the mirror.

It's Dan Moralis.

Maybe he's Brooke's plant. Or maybe he's after me for some other reason.

He's about to enter the bathroom, but then he stops. I take another deep breath. My pepper spray is ready to fire, and I don't move a muscle. I think again about letting him know I'm here.

Maybe this is all a big misunderstanding.

Maybe he's here because he offered to pack up her room, like me?

But then he whips aggressively towards me, and my instincts kick in. His hand is raised. I point at his face and depress the button on my only weapon, hoping it will be enough.

He lets out a ferocious howl as the pepper spray hits him square in the eyes. I duck down and shift to the side while he's still blinded and confused, avoiding any possible retaliation. I've had some training. I escape from the bathroom. Then I make a beeline for the apartment door and run for my life.

NINE

Cassie

I didn't have to run very far before I smacked into a security guard headed in our direction. I muttered something about Kimi's room and pepper spray, and he went running to check on Dan.

Now it's twenty minutes later, and I'm in an interrogation of sorts with Brooke, Doug Walker, and Stan, the head of security. We're in the faculty lounge inside the administration building. Dan's been taken to the ER to wash out his eyes, which seems like overkill to me. I told them I didn't know it was Dan when I sprayed him, which is a total lie of course. And that I ran to get help when I saw who it was.

"What were you thinking?" Brooke is furious with me. I don't really care, though. And it's only pepper spray. It will wear off. It's not like I shot the guy.

"I thought he was a burglar. I told you. I couldn't see who it was until after I sprayed him. Then I went for help. What was Dan doing in Kimi's room anyway?"

"What were *you* doing in Kimi's room?" Brooke shoots back. "You scared him too. He thought *you* were a burglar."

"I have a spare key. She gave it to me months ago. I was going to start packing up her things, so her parents wouldn't have to do it. I was just trying to help."

"You should have cleared that with us first, Cassie," Doug says. His tone is milder than Brooke's, but I can tell he's upset. His lips are pressed together, and I can see tension lines on his forehead.

Brooke informs me that Dan went there to get Kimi's copy of *Adventures of Huckleberry Finn*. She tells us he wanted her marked-up copy because he's never taught that book before, and now I'm even more suspicious. What English teacher hasn't taught *Adventures of Huckleberry Finn*? And how did he know it was in her room? As if reading my mind, she continues.

"We looked for the book in her office and it wasn't there, so he went to her room to look for it." Her eyes are like daggers, cutting my lie into shreds. But I'm not buying her story either. The book was sitting on the desk, so why was he looking in the drawers?

But I need to turn down the heat, so I keep my suspicions to myself. Brooke's still glaring at me, the security chief is sizing me up in silence, and Doug Walker isn't looking at any of us. Rather, he's staring off into the distance looking a little preoccupied. Maybe he's thinking about the health scare he had in the cafeteria. We've gotten no further information, but I'm sure it wasn't nothing.

"How did he get in?" I ask.

"He saw the door was open a crack, and he went in to see if the book was there," Brooke says.

I'm pretty sure I closed the door. It doesn't lock automatically, so I can't say for certain if I locked it or not.

Maybe he *was* just coming in to get the book. I don't know what to think anymore. I hate living like this, being afraid and suspicious all the time. I wish I could tell them the reason I'm always on edge. But I can't.

"I'm so sorry. I think I'm just jumpy because of what happened to Kimi. And from seeing the police here the other day."

A sympathetic look comes over Doug Walker's face. "I understand, Cassie. And now we've asked you to stay over break. But the police have assured us that what happened to Kimi was an accident. And it didn't even happen on campus. Please know that we have top-notch security in place. You're safe here. We're all safe."

I'm never safe.

But I nod and lower my eyes.

"Dan must be furious with me. I need to apologize to him." I say what they want to hear, although I don't really know what to think. I don't trust Brooke. What if she's pulling the strings and she told Dan to go in there and look for evidence of whatever Kimi had on her? Or what if I'm simply paranoid and being ridiculous?

"I don't think he's mad, Cassie." Stan, the security chief, finally says something. "He actually seemed kind of amused by it."

"Dan said he was amused? That I pepper sprayed him?" I feel my brow wrinkle.

"He said you were a feisty one," Stan replies.

Try as I might to keep my poker face on, I have to fight to stop a grin from spreading.

Dan thinks I'm feisty.

———

I'm back in my room now, and I think everything worked out okay. Everyone seemed comfortable with the assumption that it was simply a big misunderstanding, although I'm still wary of Brooke.

After an hour or so, I hear a car engine idling outside our building. Then I hear a car door slam shut. I look out the window and see Dan coming back from the ER. I decide to wait out in the hall and apologize to him. I need to face him sooner or later, so I might as well get it over with.

I open my apartment door and wait in the doorway. I hear him walking up the steps. When he comes into view, I can see even from this distance that his eyes are bloodshot. He flashes me a smirk.

If he's not in on this with Brooke, then I've pepper sprayed a really nice guy.

"Dan. I'm so sorry," I offer as he approaches. "I didn't know it was you." I'm sure he believes me. I'm a good liar. I've had lots of practice.

"It was an honest mistake."

"But…your eyes." I scan them, and they're even more red up close. "Are they okay?"

"I'll be fine. I'm just tired." His head tilts to the side as he speaks, and there's no tension in his face. No clenched jaw. No furrowed brow. And the faint hint of a smile. He doesn't seem at all upset with me, and I find this curious. Either he's a very forgiving guy, or he's got something to hide.

"Sure. Go get some sleep."

As he starts to leave, I call to him. "Oh, and Dan?"

"Yes?"

"Brooke tells me you've never taught *Adventures of Huckleberry Finn*. You should've come to me. I have tons of lesson plans I can share with you."

"I'll take you up on that. Tomorrow."

"Tomorrow it is." I wave him off and head back into my room.

I'd love to ask him why he was looking in the desk drawers when the book was sitting on top of her desk. But now is not the time. He must know I heard him do that. Maybe that's why he's not making a big deal about the incident. But why would he rummage through her drawers if there's nothing hinky going on?

Maybe it was simple curiosity. Or maybe he was looking for more class materials? If I'm being honest, I would probably be tempted to look too. And I don't get a bad vibe from him. On the contrary, he seems like a good guy, not at all like the kind of guy who would do something illegal or unethical.

But then I thought that about my own father, so what do I know?

I suppose the smart thing to do would be to check in with WITSEC and tell them what's going on. That's the program I'm in, the one charged with protecting me. It's run by the federal marshal service. They're quite proud of the fact that they've never lost a witness or family member since its inception in the early seventies. At least the ones who've followed their rules. They made sure to drive that point home to us when my family entered the program seventeen years ago.

At first, they were a visible presence in our lives, when we disappeared from our suburban home just outside Las Vegas and tried to blend into our equally generic and innocuous suburban home in Sacramento. But now we only check in with them a few times a year unless we have cause for concern.

I could make contact and tell them about the SUV that may or may not have been following me the other day. And then I could come clean about Kimi's letter and my suspicions. This isn't the first time I've felt I was being followed. It happened once in college when I'd just started freshman year. Only it wasn't a dark green SUV. It was a silver Chevy sedan.

It turned out I *was* being followed. By my WITSEC handler. She was checking up on me in my new location.

Transitions make people vulnerable, she said. Not to mention large quantities of alcohol, which is why I'm always careful to never drink to excess. I tried to assure her there was nothing to worry about. But she and I had become pretty close. She was quite protective of me. But she's since moved on.

I have a new agent now, someone I don't know very well, so I'm not crazy about the idea of reaching out to him. I don't want them to get all skittish and overreact. They might try to convince us that we need to disappear all over again, especially if they thought I was in danger.

Ironically, my father insists he didn't give up anything too incriminating as part of his deal with the feds. He was indicted on a money laundering charge in the wake of September 11th when the Patriot Act was in full force and they were hunting for terrorists. He and his buddies got picked up in a sweep. He was allegedly fencing stolen merchandise for some mob guy, a family friend who didn't even get jail time as part of his eventual conviction.

My father claimed he didn't know the merchandise was stolen, a position he maintains to this day. But the mob guy was connected to a wider network of people that may have included a terrorist cell, so there was a chance we were in real danger. My dad felt it was better to take the fresh start the feds were offering. In hindsight, I suppose he was probably right.

I weigh the pros and cons of involving WITSEC at this point, and I decide against it. If I really feel like I'm in danger, I can always have them come to my rescue. That thought gives me some peace of mind for now. But I can't just let this go. I owe it to Kimi to try to figure out what's going on. And I have to admit that my curiosity is piqued.

Because although I don't get a dangerous vibe from Dan, I still can't shake the feeling that there's more to the guy than meets the eye. I need to spend more time with him. Get to know him. And then a thought pops into my head, although I kind of wish it hadn't.

How hard would it be to sneak into his room and have a look around?

TEN

Cassie

jiggle the paperclip in the slot, but I can't quite reach the tumbler to engage it.

This is a bad idea.

I've done this before, many times, but it's been a while. Thankfully, this is an older building. The lock is child's play for anyone with even a rudimentary idea of how to do this. They were planning to tear this structure down and build a new one. But then the school ran into financial trouble. It's still scheduled to be demolished though, so there's no motivation to do much maintenance on it.

Contrary to the student dorm, which is a state-of-the-art fortress, the faculty residential building is a tempting invitation for burglars and psychopaths. There are no cameras and the building itself isn't secure. There's only a simple doorknob lock on our apartment doors to keep people out of our units. There's a deadbolt, but it needs to be engaged from inside the apartment, so we're at least a bit more protected when we're in our units.

Breaking into this apartment when it's empty should be a no-brainer for me. And this lock shouldn't be giving me so much trouble. But my hands are shaking. And the latex gloves I'm wearing are hampering my dexterity a bit. I don't have much time, and that's stressing me out. I stop. I take a deep breath in. I let a slow breath out. Then I try again.

I hear a click and turn the knob.

Presto. I'm in.

Everyone's at the Christmas concert. I was there too, but I sat at the back and ducked out when the first number started. I've got about twenty minutes to snoop around. I saw Dan near the front of the auditorium. It would be hard for him to leave the way he's sandwiched in, and we're the only two who live on this floor, so I'm pretty sure I won't get caught. I just need to be quick.

I learned to pick locks from my father, whose major fear was that someone might kidnap me and hold me somewhere to try to get at him. I don't know if I come by my claustrophobia naturally or if it is the result of envisioning being locked in a room somewhere, trapped and helpless. That thought terrifies me more than being shot to death. He even had me practice getting myself out of a car trunk.

Heartwarming childhood memories.

I look around and take inventory. His room has the same layout as mine. It's a studio, with a small kitchenette to the left, a desk and loveseat near the door, a sleeping area with a bed, dresser, and nightstand in the far corner, and a bathroom off the bedroom. It's very sparsely decorated, which I suppose makes sense. With all his moving around, he seems like the kind of guy who would travel light.

The book he took from Kimi's room sits on his desk, and there's a backpack on the chair in front of it. I walk farther in and notice the bed is unmade but tidy. The bedding is turned down and folded over into a neat triangle awaiting his return, as if he's the kind of sleeper who doesn't toss and turn too much and simply slips out of bed without disturbing it. I see no personal effects—no family photos, no wall hangings, no nicknacks—no hints about who this guy really is or what his personality is like.

I dig around in his backpack, which is fairly empty. I pull out a folder that contains some personnel documents. There's an address and some other background information on one of the documents. With my phone, I quickly snap some photos. There's nothing of further value, so I move on.

I walk over to the closet and open it. His clothes hang in perfect symmetry with equal space between the hangers. The shirts are organized according to type: polos, dress shirts, and sweaters. His pants, naturally, inhabit their own territory on the opposite side of the closet. The shoes are lined up in formation on the closet floor.

Maybe he's former military? Or he has OCD?

I feel a pang of guilt as I consider the latter. If he's simply a nice guy with a right to privacy and not a danger to our community, I'm a terrible person for invading his space.

I move into the bathroom, and there are no surprises there. Toothpaste, toothbrush, razor, soap, deodorant, and a bottle of Axe body wash in the shower. I think back on his manly scent and go a little weak in the knees in spite of myself. No aftershave, as I suspected. And no contact lens solution. He must have great vision, because he doesn't wear glasses. I check the drawers and they're all empty. Then I exit the bathroom.

I head over to his bed and look under it. Nothing's there. On the nightstand, there's a Kindle and a digital clock radio with an iPhone charger attached to it. I check my watch and realize I need to get going. I pull open the top drawer of the nightstand a bit too forcefully, expecting it to be empty, and I hear a clunk.

My head is spinning as I struggle to process what I'm seeing, and I'm seized with an overwhelming desire to run out of his room. Instead, I pick up the object and examine it. It's a Glock 17.

Oh my God. Who is this guy?

Thanks to my father, I know my weapons pretty well, and I know how to handle one, although I refuse to have one in my home. I snap a photo, put the gun back, and close the drawer. I realize now that I've wanted to be wrong about him. But obviously, I'm not. And I have no idea what to do next. Besides get out of his room and back to the concert before I get caught.

———

I crack open the door to the auditorium and peek in. A soloist is performing "Silent Night," and it's pretty quiet. I feel like it would be conspicuous if I enter now. I decide I'll wait for the end of the number and head in when the applause starts.

"Hey, Cass," Ed whispers from behind me.

I startle and my head whips around towards him. "I...um..."

He smiles, likely sensing my discomfort. If he only knew what I was really up to.

"Don't worry. I'm just getting here too. Nobody cares," he offers.

"I went to the bathroom," I whisper back.

The applause starts and we rush in to find seats. I part ways from Ed, dart over to the far side of the last row, and sit down. I imagine he'll be a bit hurt that I ditched him, but I'm too frazzled to be around him now. I know I said I was a good liar, but not to people I really care about. And he's becoming a genuine friend.

It's been nearly impossible for me to get truly close to people over the years, and I'm sure that contributed to my recent breakup. With Evan, there was always a barrier between us—the part of my life I could never share with him—and he commented more than a few times about my being distant. I wonder how I'll ever find true love and connection when I can't even tell someone who I really am.

The only silver lining in all of the upheaval is that I got to keep my first name, so I'm still Cassie. I insisted on it, and the feds thought it wouldn't be too much of a risk. They convinced my parents that it might even lessen the chances of my screwing up, so they'd finally agreed to it. At some point, I suppose I'm going to have to trust someone enough to tell them the whole story.

But how will I know when it's safe?

It's getting towards the end of the concert because I see Erin Kensington going up to the stage. I remember from the program that her solo was the second-to-last number. I met with her mother last week, briefly, and she was down-to-earth, as Ed assured me that she would be. She confirmed what Ed said. She'd worked in education for a while before Erin was born. And she seemed to have respect for teachers, unlike some people at her economic and social level.

She informed me that Erin's been having some boyfriend troubles, some guy who doesn't go to our school, and that likely accounted for her troubled emotional state. We agreed that it would probably sort itself out over winter break, and I told her I'd keep her posted if anything was amiss second semester. I figure that might be a lie, about Erin and the boy troubles. Her daughter might actually be upset by the rumor floating around, even if it's not true. But, of course, I didn't let on about that. It's none of my business, and I'm happy to accept her mother's explanation and move on.

Erin walks onstage and stands up straighter as if she's been trained to do so. She takes a deep breath. And then she starts.

A long, sweet, and haunting *ahhhhhh* rings out in perfect pitch, and everyone in the auditorium sits up a bit higher as if rising up to meet it. Her voice is clear and sweet as she continues with her rendition of "Ave Maria."

Her performance is truly flawless as if an angel had come down from heaven to sing for us. I'm completely floored. There's an emotional depth to her performance that seems to come from deep within her being. It actually brings tears to my eyes. And that's really saying something because I'm usually not much for this sort of thing.

When she stops, the audience is perfectly still for a bit, as if they're trying to process what they've just heard. Then I see someone in the front stand up. Soon the crowd is giving her a standing ovation. After the applause dies down, the final group of students comes on stage. *I would not want to follow her.*

The group starts on a fun and lively rendition of "Santa Claus Is Coming to Town," which is perfect. It lightens the mood after those two heavy numbers, something we all need. Everyone claps along, and the concert ends on a festive, happy note.

When they finish their song, Doug Walker takes the stage and thanks the music teacher, the students, and the guests. Then he wishes everyone a happy and safe winter break. We're getting up to leave when we see his eyes pop open. One hand goes to his chest, and the other grasps the podium. Gasps echo through the chamber.

"Doug!" Brooke Baxter calls out. She rushes to the stage as Walker tumbles to the wooden floor and lands with a thundering thud. "Call nine-one-one," she yells to the crowd.

"I've got it," someone yells back.

Dan Moralis bolts up to the stage. More people start to stand up, including me. Dan starts performing CPR as we wait for the ambulance. My heart races, and I think about going up there and pushing him aside. What if he's doing it wrong, trying to finish him off?

But that's crazy. Everyone's watching him.

I'm starting to wish I never got that letter and that I never went into his room. But I can't unsee what I saw. I hear sirens in the distance as I consider my options. And the most attractive one is to quit and get away from this place as fast as I can.

ELEVEN

Miles

I stare at the stage in total disbelief as the paramedics arrive and go to work on Doug Walker. My head is throbbing and I feel like I need to get some air. Listening to my daughter's haunting rendition of "Ave Maria" just a short while ago, the purity of her voice nearly moved me to tears, contrasting sharply with the bitter build-up of guilt that's starting to strangle me.

I'm a lapsed Catholic, and Erin's notes brought me right back to my childhood days, with my devout parents insisting I repent for my sins on a weekly basis. Now I'm starting to feel like my head will explode if I don't kneel down and confess.

And then a really crazy thought pops into my head.

What if I somehow willed this to happen?

And then another, more plausible one.

What if I'm descending into madness?

But then I look over at my wife and daughter beside me and decide that neither confession nor madness is a viable option. I put my arm around Erin, who is visibly shaken. Madeline squeezes my arm, and I reach over and kiss her on the head. They need me, and all these mental musings are unproductive. Doug Walker had a heart issue before he even came to work here, so this is simply an unfortunate occurrence, and the fact that I feel guilty at all is a sign that I'm not a bad person, just a guy with his back against the wall who made some bad decisions.

It looks like Walker is doing better, and we watch without a word as the paramedics take him away.

Erin finally breaks the silence. "I don't want to stay at Sara's house tonight. And I don't want to drive right now, Mom." Tears are welling up in her eyes.

"I'll go with you and drive your car, honey. Dad probably needs to stay here for a while anyway."

"Probably. Yeah. You two go. I'll catch up with you later."

They turn to leave, but I call out to them. "Erin?"

"What?" She whips her head around as if she's annoyed by the delay.

"You were wonderful tonight, sweetie. I'm so sorry it ended like this. But that doesn't change the fact that you were wonderful. And I'm so proud of you."

She comes over and hugs me, and I kiss the top of her head. I can feel a few tears soaking into my shirt. We stay like that for a while, and I'm grateful for this rare tender moment with my sweet little daddy's girl from years ago.

Then she straightens up and takes a deep breath. "Thanks, Dad. See you later."

———

Brooke and I are on better terms these days. I don't know for sure why she had a change of heart, but it might have something to do with the fact that she's not getting interviews anywhere else. We've settled into a truce of sorts, and it's working. For now.

And now that I have a possible opportunity to make good on my promise to deliver the head of school job, at least temporarily, it puts me in a stronger position. Interim head of school is better than nothing, and it could give Brooke a chance to prove herself and fix my problem. But it's too soon to go public with my idea. It would look callous. Still, I need to make sure she's on board.

Most people have left, except for the two of us and the cleaning crew. Brooke is sitting on the stage with her head in her hands, looking exhausted. Now I'm starting to feel bad about my suspicions. According to the authorities, the teacher died of a slip and fall, and I could kick myself for voicing my concerns to Brooke. It was likely just a co-incidence that she expressed concerns about Kimi being onto us a few days before her death. I shouldn't have gone there. Just because Brooke's ambitious doesn't mean she's a murderer.

I walk over and sit down next to her on the stage. "How are you holding up?" I ask.

She tilts her head to the side, looks over at me, and sighs. "I've been better."

"I know it's a little premature to discuss this. But if he's...if Walker...um...needs some time for his recovery, how would you feel about stepping up? As interim head?"

She rolls her eyes. "Should we even be talking about this now? He's barely out the door, Miles."

"It's my job to keep the school stable, Brooke."

"That's not how I wanted to get it. I wanted to win. Fair and square." She shakes her head.

"I know you did."

Without thinking, I put a hand on her shoulder and then promptly remove it, not wanting to fuel more speculation.

"So, is that a 'no'?"

"No. It's not a no." She pauses for a moment. "Of course I'll do it. If it comes to that. I just don't think we should be talking about it. Not yet."

"We need to be prepared. I'll assess the situation when we have more information, and we'll make a decision from there. But I need to know that you're ready to step in if needed. I'll probably call a board meeting tomorrow or as soon as we know more."

She nods. "I'm ready."

"I know you are. And don't feel guilty about taking advantage of this opportunity. It's not your fault. He's had a heart condition for years. Sometimes things just happen, and nobody can blame you for making the most of a bad situation. And for stepping up and keeping the school going."

And no one can blame me, either.

TWELVE

Cassie

Something is very wrong here. I can feel it. They took Doug away about an hour ago. I'm back in my apartment, lying on my bed, kicking myself for not taking action earlier. I should have gone to the police in person with that letter. Now I'll never know what became of it, and the curiosity is killing me.

What if it got stuffed in a file somewhere by a clerk and didn't get to the right people? What if there's some truth to what Kimi said in it, but nobody will ever know? And how can I make this right?

I still feel guilty that I didn't make time to actually talk to Kimi when she asked me to meet up with her, and I'm disappointed in myself for getting caught up in the gossip and petty politics of this place. I should have been stronger, but then I'm terrible at this stuff. Ripped away from my social circle at a young age, I never quite fit in after that.

Most of the time I feel like an outsider wherever I go, but with Kimi I found a measure of kinship. Maybe it was because she was iced out by the other faculty members and I have trouble making friends—the two unpopular girls sitting at the misfit lunch table. She must have felt terrible when I started to pull back. I should at least try to get her concerns on the right person's radar.

And what should I do about Dan? I can't very well report that he has a gun in his room without admitting to breaking and entering. I really backed myself into a corner on that one, and I'm struggling to find a way out of it. When they took Doug Walker away tonight, he looked a bit better, so maybe there's hope for him, and for us, because losing a head of school now would be a total disaster for our community and our morale. I can't help connecting the dots, though, and I don't like the picture that's emerging.

First, Kimi's concerned about Brooke Baxter plotting against Doug Walker. Then Kimi falls down the stairs and dies. Next, I get a cryptic letter saying that Brooke Baxter is plotting against Doug Walker. Then a teacher arrives out of nowhere to take Kimi's place, and he just happens to have a Glock in his room. And finally, Walker collapses on the last day of school.

But then I look at it from the opposite perspective, as if they are all isolated incidents. Kimi has suspicions about Brooke Baxter, ones she wanted to tell me about. She's nervous and stressed, and she slips and falls down the stairs. They find a replacement for her pretty quickly, a guy who has a sick grandmother in the vicinity. Then Doug Walker, who has a heart condition we all know about, collapses.

All unfortunate but unrelated incidents.

I can almost buy this, except for the gun. I'm pretty sure he can't have a gun on a school campus. But then, it's his personal residence, and people can have guns in their homes. Maybe it's perfectly legal. I should do some research.

But first, I need a break. And I need to get my mind off this.

So I start scrolling through the photos on my phone. I haven't deleted the last few of Evan and me, but I decide that now is as good a time as any for a fresh start.

Delete.

Delete.

Delete.

Then I come across some photos of my parents, and my mind wanders back to better times, to my early childhood before my world changed, although none of those images are on this phone. We didn't have phones like this back then.

I remember feeling content as a kid, if a little bored. After everything happened, I would sometimes beat myself up for not appreciating what I had at the time. I wanted adventures, but before the great disruption, most of mine were fictional, confined to my young adult mystery and romance novels or the occasional excursion to somewhere more exciting than our little suburb. Little did I know I'd soon be missing our boring, predictable routine.

The development where we lived, a few miles outside of Las Vegas, was a perfectly nice place to raise children. But it was dull, especially for an only child. I lived for our family excursions to the Vegas Strip, where every day was like Christmas, with its bright lights and pulsating energy.

But that was nothing compared to the first time we visited Manhattan. I was about nine, I think, and we did the whole Christmas tourist thing: ice-skated at Rockefeller Center, saw *Wicked*, and went to see the Rockettes at Radio City. We ate, we shopped, and we trekked around the city for hours and hours. I was in heaven.

And now I feel an ache in the pit of my being, a loneliness that's seeping into every corner of my body. I understand now how people can literally die from loneliness. Maybe my relationship with Evan wasn't perfect, but at least I had someone in my life at this time last year. And if

I'd stayed in San Diego, I could walk around the city, try to meet new people. The sheer isolation of this place is killing me. It's creepy and sad and cold, and I've never felt so alone.

I'm seized with a rare urge to connect with the two people in the world who know me best. The two people in the world who know who I really am. It's just after nine in the evening here, but it's only dinnertime in California. I pick up my phone, scroll down, and tap a button. My mom picks up after two rings as if she's been glancing down at her phone since the last time we spoke a few weeks ago, waiting for some word from me.

"Cassie! Is something wrong?" She knows me well, and I usually check in on Sunday afternoons. A call on a Saturday evening is a red flag.

"No. Not really. I just wanted to say hi."

"Cassie?" From her tone, I know she's not buying it.

I go on to tell her what happened to Doug Walker. My dad's had some heart issues too, so she assumes that I'm worried about him and I'm reaching out because the incident made me think of him. I suppose I should be concerned about my dad, and I feel terrible for not making the connection. Still, I pretend that's what I'm concerned about because I don't feel comfortable talking about the real issues over an unsecured phone line. If I decide to tell my parents about what's going on, I'll need to do it in person.

"Your dad's been doing great, sweetie. Don't worry about him. But we'd really like to see you for Christmas. Can't you try to swing by after your Florida trip? We'll cover the cost."

I realize that a lot has happened since I last talked to her. I fill her in on the fact that the Florida trip has been postponed since I'm now required to stay over winter break, and I've been promoted to department chair. She congratulates me and then makes a suggestion I would have rejected last week but that suddenly sounds very appealing.

"What if we come to New York to see you?"

This would be perfect, actually. I can talk to my parents in person. Tell them everything. And we can decide what to do from there. Maybe we could even stay in the city for a night or two, and I could get a break from this place. As if reading my mind, she continues.

"We'll treat you to a night or two in the city. Just like old times."

I feel my heart start to warm at the thought, and I know that I need to find a way to start forgiving my father. Resentment is toxic, and I'm not a child anymore. But it's so hard. He was my world before all this happened, and our entire relationship changed that day.

My mother is quite serious, and she played the heavy in the family. She's the one who bandaged my scraped knees and made sure I did my homework and the one who grounded me when I screwed up. My dad was the fun parent. The one who tickled me and made funny faces when I was little. And the one who made me laugh when I felt like crying.

I'll never forget the look of shame on his face that night when I sat on the sofa sobbing. It was my mother who comforted me. My dad couldn't even look at me. I said horrible things to him, and I'm certain that my words ripped into him and filled him with guilt and remorse. It's never been the same since then, although we both try. But what used to be effortless now feels awkward and forced, and I don't know how to get back to where we once were.

"Hang on a minute. Your dad wants to say hi." She doesn't give me a choice.

"Hi, Cass. How're you doing out there? Cold enough for you?"

"It's freezing. And they're chintzy on the heat in my room too."

"Cheap bastards!"

I smile. And then I lie. I don't know why. "It's not that bad. You get used to it."

"I guess we'll get a taste of it. Your mom tells me we're headed your way."

The fact that my parents are willing to drop everything the minute I decide to grace them with my presence should make me feel guilty about how little I give of myself to them, but it doesn't. Maybe someday it will, but not yet.

We wrap up our call and it's all settled. They'll fly in on Christmas, just in time to officially spend it with me, and stay through New Year's Day. I'll get more details about my duty schedule over break, and we'll land on some dates when I can stay in the city with them.

I love Manhattan at Christmas, and I'm actually very excited about this little getaway. I'll finally be able to come clean to my parents and get some advice about what to do next. I just need to get through the first week here alone.

How hard can that be?

THIRTEEN

Cassie

I'm feeling a bit better today. It's Sunday morning, and we've heard nothing further about Doug Walker, so I'm assuming he's doing okay. The facilities people even got around to cutting back the tree branches, so I'm sleeping better. I finish up my toast, fill up my water bottle, and head over to the gym.

It's warmed up a little today, and when the air hits my face it feels crisp rather than frigid; the sensation invigorates me. I'm on duty today, and we're taking the kids on a field trip this afternoon to Sunnyside, Washington Irving's retreat on the Hudson. I'm looking forward to seeing it.

The sky is a clear powder blue. I stop at the edge of the ridge to admire the Hudson River sparkling in the distance, beyond the jagged mountain peaks, the evergreens adding a splash of color to the winter landscape. It actually looks kind of beautiful to me right now, and I wonder if that's because I'm excited to see my parents. Maybe it always looks like this, but I just don't see it most of the time, when I'm mired in negativity. I take a deep breath, take it all in, and let myself feel positive about life for a few rare moments before I get on my way.

But all my concerns come rushing back when I open the door to the faculty gym and Dan whips his head around towards me. It's a pretty small space with a few cardio machines and some free weights, so we're going to have to interact. I was already a little nervous around him, before my snooping, and now I have to pretend that I wasn't in his room. And that I don't know he has a Glock in his nightstand.

He's curling his weights, standing there staring at me with a curious look on his face.

As if he can read my mind.

I feel my pulse start to race a bit.

"Hi, Cassie," he says.

A thin black nylon workout shirt hugs his upper body, showing off a fine pair of pecs, and his biceps bulge as he continues his reps. What high school English teacher has a body like his? He looks more like a Navy SEAL. Or a fireman. I've already gotten a few complaints from some of the better seniors about his teaching. They said he's a nice guy but "clueless" and they're worried about their AP scores.

I need to talk to Brooke about the possibility of switching him out of the more challenging classes, but we're understaffed and we don't have many alternatives for teachers. I asked her why she didn't vet him more thoroughly, and she said he was hired at the insistence of Doug Walker and came with glowing references. I'm not sure I believe her, but I can't very well challenge her or go over her head and ask Doug Walker myself. And I suppose it's my job to get him acclimated, so she'll just throw it all back on me.

"Hey, Dan. How are you?"

"I'm good," he says. "And you?"

Most English teachers say *I'm well.*

It can be annoying to people outside our world, but that's what we say. I censor myself in certain settings so I don't sound too bookish, but to another English teacher, it's sort of a calling card. But Dan's "good" today, and I decide I need to do more research into this guy. When I get back to my room, I'll start digging into those personnel documents I photographed. I'm no computer genius though, so I'm not too sure I'll find anything even if there is something to find. But I'll give it a try.

"I'm fine," I reply.

I head over to the elliptical, wishing I'd brought earbuds. I'm usually the only one in here, so I'm free to play my music out loud. Now I'll have to work out in silence. Plus, it's really awkward with only the two of us here, and I can't hide from him without my buds.

"You work out a lot?" he asks.

"I work out often. But not a lot." I'm toying with him now, and it's fun. I fight to suppress a smile.

"Huh?"

"I mean, I work out frequently. But not excessively." I'm challenging him to some wordplay, but he's not engaging.

"Oh." I think I see the hint of a smirk on his face. *I better stop. If he really is Brooke's plant, I can't let on that I'm onto him.*

"Anyway," he continues, "have you heard anything about Doug?"

"No, but I'm assuming no news is good news."

"Fair assumption."

"I'll let all of you know right away if I hear anything."

"Thanks."

I'm about to start up my cardio session when I turn to him one more time. "Dan?"

"Yes, Cassie?"

"What you did last night? That was…you may have saved Doug's life. We're all grateful. Thank you."

"It was nothing. My instincts kicked in."

"Your instincts?"

"I worked my way through grad school as a paramedic."

"Oh. Wow."

Now I'm the one with the stunted vocabulary. I have to admit, it's a bit of a turn-on, thinking about my hunky next-door neighbor as a lifesaving superhero.

A lifesaving superhero with a gun.

He's going to get suspicious if I pry any further, so I shut the conversation down. "Good to have you on board, Dan."

I start up my machine and its loud hum envelops me. At some point, I hear the door to the gym open and shut. When I turn around to look, he's gone.

I'm in my room now, looking over the photos of the documents I found in his backpack. There's no resume, just an address in Croton-on-Hudson, a town about twenty minutes south of here. Maybe that's his parents' house. Or his grandmother's.

I do an internet search to find his social media. There's no LinkedIn profile, but I locate his Facebook page, and it's pretty sparse. There's a profile picture of him on a mountain bike and some photos of him at the school in Guatemala that Brooke mentioned when she introduced him. He's got just over fifty friends, which doesn't seem like much, but I can't see them. Most of his page is private, so that's about all I'm going to get. I wonder how hard it is to hack into someone's private page and who might have the skills to pull off something like that. Certainly not me.

I'm interrupted by an alert on my phone, and I feel a tingling in my scalp. There's an emergency meeting in twenty minutes, and I can't imagine it's good news. But then maybe I feel that way because this seems so familiar in the wake of the announcement about Kimi's death. Perhaps Doug is fine and the news is that he's taking some time off.

I head into the shower to get ready to walk over, hoping for the best but preparing for the worst.

———

I enter the auditorium a bit later than everyone else. I don't see Ed, but I do see Dan. I position myself so I can keep an eye on him. Many of the faculty members left this morning for winter break, and those of us remaining are spread out in the seats. Most of the students are leaving today too, aside from the handful who are boarding over break, the ones we're staying behind to supervise. I feel a little isolated, and I'm really happy my parents are coming.

Brooke Baxter and Miles Kensington are on the stage. They're off to the side, huddled together in close conversation, and if I didn't know any better, I'd assume from their body language they were a bit more than business associates. They seem to be in the midst of figuring out how to handle this meeting. After a bit, they notice the crowd and snap into action. Brooke takes the podium and thanks us for coming, and then she turns it over to the board chair. He apologizes for the inconvenience. Then he delivers some terrible news.

He tells us that Doug suffered a massive heart attack in the ambulance and died at the hospital. I'm absolutely devastated, and I can see from my vantage point a sea of faces with open mouths and raised eyebrows reacting to the news. All except one.

Dan's face is immobile a few seconds longer than the others before it registers the requisite look of shock and disbelief.

Sort of like he already knew.

———

We're just arriving at our field trip destination, Washington Irving's residence on the Hudson, and I wonder how long it will take until the students figure out that something's up. We were instructed not to tell the students about Doug Walker until there's more information on how it will be handled internally and who will replace him.

Plus, they want the students to have a pleasant holiday, so they don't want to send them off on long plane rides with another death on their minds. It might be hard to keep it from the ones who are staying over break. News tends to seep out in this kind of environment.

Ed and I are the chaperones, and we only have three students with us, the three who are staying over break. Marko, my Ukrainian junior, Bai, a junior boy from China, and Lily, a sophomore girl from South Korea. Ed drove us in his Camry sedan, and it was a cozy ride. It's about a forty-minute drive, and we didn't talk much, which was fine with me. The kids have different native tongues, and I'm guessing they might need a break from using English all the time. I wonder if they feel sad about being left behind. Marko's a scholarship student and his home is a war zone. I get that, but I'm curious about the other two and why they're not going home.

We arrive a bit early and stroll around the grounds, and I'm dying to ask Ed what he thinks about Doug Walker's death. I wonder if anyone aside from me is concerned, or connecting the dots at all. He doesn't know about Kimi's letter or what she suspected. And he doesn't know what I know about Dan. If I didn't know, would I simply accept both incidents as unfortunate occurrences?

The residence is strikingly beautiful in its simplicity. It looks like something out of a fairy tale, like it could be made of gingerbread. But it's just a house on a large lot on the bank of the Hudson and nothing else. There's not much to do while we wait on the grounds for our tour to start. I was hoping there would be a gift shop or something that would distract the students so Ed and I could get some time alone, but there's not.

Then an opportunity presents itself.

"Ms. Romano?" Marko says.

"Yes?"

"We want to walk there, down to the river. It's okay?"

"Sure. Just be back in fifteen minutes."

The three of them go on their way, and I turn to Ed. "So, what do you think of the news this morning?"

"What do I think?" His brow furrows. "I think it's sad. What do you mean?"

"It's just, Kimi and now Doug Walker? Doesn't it seem… strange?"

"What are you getting at, Cassie?" His tone is sharp and his jaw is tight.

He's never looked at me like this before. Maybe he's offended by the idea of my spinning this into something sordid or sensational, like I'm being a gossip. I remember that he came to Brooke Baxter's defense the last time we talked about the head of school feud and the rumor about her and Miles Kensington. I decide I need to shut this down. I don't need him turning on me.

"Nothing. It's nothing. It's just sad, that's all," I say.

Ed's face softens a bit, and he nods. "It's a lot to process, I'm sure. And she was a friend of yours."

"Yes," I reply. "She was."

We pass the time geeking out about Washington Irving and his place in American literature until the students return and the tour begins. It's actually very engaging, and for a time, I focus on the guide who takes us around the modest but surprisingly modern-looking structure with its white walls and its ahead-of-its-time skylight. It looks like a great place to write and think. The woman entertains us with tales of his lingering spirit, which still makes the occasional appearance; he died in his bedroom, right in this house, after all. And that brings me back to reality.

Death.

The death of two people I know, at my workplace, in the space of a few weeks. I wish I hadn't said anything to Ed about my morbid suspicions, because there's a distance between us that wasn't there before. I was starting to think of him as a father figure, but this is a wake-up call. I don't know him very well, and I need to fix what's broken in my own family, not seek out a surrogate one. The drive back is awkward, the silence no longer comfortable, and I feel more alone than I ever have.

The thought of seeing my parents had been lifting my spirits, but when I think about them going back to California, about facing the long, frigid, isolating winter alone on that mountain after they leave, a cloud of sadness settles over me. It doesn't help that the day has turned stormy. A light sprinkle of raindrops dots the windshield, and the wipers squeak as they scrape back and forth across the damp surface.

I don't think I can wait until June. It feels like an eternity. The loneliness will kill me. The hell with the consequences. I'm quitting this job and going back to Sacramento with my parents.

FOURTEEN

Cassie

It's been pretty quiet the last few days since we got the terrible news about Doug. We've been rotating our days on duty—each of us takes a twenty-four-hour period with the students—so I haven't seen much of Dan or Ed, even with Dan living next door. This schedule allows us to go off campus on our days off. I figure maybe Dan is visiting his sick grandmother, if he was even telling the truth about that.

My parents are coming soon, and we've booked two nights in the city for my days off. I wonder how they'll react to all of my happenings, especially the news that I'm going to be moving in with them, at least temporarily. I expect they'll be thrilled.

When we're on duty, we sleep in the faculty quarters over at the student dorm. The faculty members who normally reside there are on vacation. It's Wednesday morning, the first week of break, and I've just finished my day on. Ed took over for me, and now I'm back in my apartment with two free days ahead of me.

I suppose things are back to normal with Ed, but I'm not sure. We haven't spoken too much since the field trip, but our interaction this morning felt pretty comfortable, not awkward like the drive home the other day. Maybe it was my imagination. We haven't talked any further about going into the city or made any definite plans, but then he knows my parents are coming, so he probably figures I'll get my fill with them. Besides, my friendship with Ed is not going to be an issue much longer, because I'm busily planning my exit from this place.

I don't have a lot of stuff to pack because I left most of my belongings at my parents' house. I can fit everything I have in one big suitcase and my carry-on bag. I haven't decided how or when I'm going to give my notice. Before I moved here last August, I sold my car and bought a new one when I arrived, one that's better in the snow. I'll have to drive it back to California. I'm planning to take the southern route because I still don't want to drive in the snow if I can avoid it.

I'm thinking I'll give my notice when I leave for the city to meet my parents in a few days. Then I'll just pack up my car, head to the city, and never come back. That will give them a week or so to find a new teacher. I feel a little bad abandoning my students, but I don't feel safe here. I have no choice. I have to go. When I get to a place where I feel more secure, I'll contact my WITSEC handler, tell him what I've uncovered, and let him decide what to do next. And in the meantime, I'm looking forward to finally unburdening myself to my parents.

Just a few more days.

I'm walking around town, and I'm starting to think I might be losing it. I thought I saw that dark green SUV again, and maybe I did.

But so what?

Maybe it belongs to someone who lives here. It didn't appear to be following me this time. It's a little on the colder side today, probably below freezing, but the sun is out and it's very bright, with the rays reflecting off the remaining patches of snow. Perhaps that's why I don't feel cold, or it could be the fact that my pulse is racing and I'm anxious, so my body temperature is elevated.

I'm headed to the bank to close out my account. I don't have my paycheck deposited there. It goes to my California checking account. But I opened a small savings account here in case I needed a physical bank. It's the only one in town, and they don't have branches in California, so there's no reason to keep it since I'm leaving forever.

The town is compact and walkable, but not very quaint, like the river towns on the other side of the Hudson, and I won't miss it. Because there's no rail line, it doesn't have the convenience to New York City for commuters, and there are not many large employers nearby. It's a working-class town, and the people are friendly and down-to-earth.

It feels pretty safe, but it's not very exciting. There's a CVS, a diner, a pizza shop, a few decent restaurants, a hair salon, and a bar, but no art galleries or boutiques, not much to do to pass the time. The one saving grace is a trendy coffee shop that displays art on its walls that serves as a nice place to chill when I want to get away from campus. I decide to go in and treat myself to a cafe latte.

The smell of freshly roasted coffee and the bright reds and greens of the Christmas decorations make me smile. I get in line to order, and I decide I'll also spring for a pump-kin scone, one with some nice, sugary icing on it that I can almost taste when I spy it in the pastry case.

It's a bit busier than usual—the ten tables are about half full—but mostly with single people, except for what looks like a mom and tween daughter at one of them, glued to their devices in comfortable silence. Soft, jazzy Christmas tunes play in the background at just the right volume.

This is just what I need right now.

I wish I brought my Kindle because I feel like I could sit and read for a bit. There's no rush to get back. But then I realize I can use my phone to start plotting out my drive home. Maybe I can find some places I want to visit on the way and make this into an adventure, something to look forward to.

After I've gotten served, I sit down with my latte and scone and start to research some cross-country routes. It looks like I could do it in eight or nine nights comfortably, although I could take longer if I want. The thought of vagabonding across the continent sounds rather exciting after being cooped up on this campus for the last few months.

I'll stop in San Diego before I head to Sacramento. It would be fun to see some of my old friends. I'm not sure I want to move back there, so I can explore alternatives along the way home. Sacramento will only be temporary, and much will depend on where I can get a job. One thing is for sure. It won't be somewhere with harsh winters.

For the route back, Asheville, North Carolina, looks like a great first stop. It's about a ten-hour drive south. I've always wanted to see that town. Then I can head west on Route 40, the most direct route across the continent. I wouldn't mind stopping in Memphis and visiting Graceland. I've seen so much of Vegas Elvis, it would be nice to experience something more authentic.

After that, the only places that really interest me are Albuquerque and Sedona. I love the desert, and I've been thinking about alternatives to California. I can do some exploring in New Mexico and Arizona on my way home; both of those states are at the top of my list.

After ten minutes or so of searching, I look up and see a guy in his mid-thirties at a table kitty-corner to me, facing my direction. Either he's checking me out or he just happened to look over here when I looked up. He's not as good-looking as Dan, but he's not bad. I feel a little flutter in my stomach, and it makes me feel alive again. It's been a while since I've played the field, and I'm eager to get back in the game.

I don't need that kind of complication now, of course, so I don't engage with him. But even the thought of meeting someone and getting on with my life sooner rather than later is enough to make me realize I'm making the right decision. I'm totally wasting my time here, and I'm excited to move on. With the teacher shortage, I might even be able to find some temporary work this year. And even if I don't, I'll land on my feet. I always do.

After a bit, I get up to leave. But as I head out the front door, I abruptly turn back because I realize I should probably use the bathroom before I go to the bank, and I almost run into the guy who was checking me out. He looks a bit annoyed, even a little angry, and my stomach tenses.

Was he planning to follow me?

But then he catches himself and smiles at me. I probably startled him when I turned around so abruptly.

"Excuse me," I say. "I forgot something."

He holds the door open for me. "After you."

I smile and thank him, and he goes on his way. I head for the restroom, shaking my head. *I need to stop letting my imagination get the best of me.*

When I'm done, I exit the coffee shop once again and head to the bank to close out my account. With my business taken care of, I enter the side alley that leads to the lot behind the buildings where my car is parked. When I get about midway down the alley, I hear footsteps behind me, and I whip my head around.

It's him.

The coffee shop guy.

I speed up, trying to get to the end of the alleyway and out into the open parking area. My heart is racing and there's a pounding in my ears. I'm almost there, but I feel like he's catching up to me. Although I can't see any other people in the lot yet, I'm confident that I'll be safer there. It was about a quarter full when I parked, so there's bound to be other people in it. And he won't do anything to me in broad daylight.

Will he?

But just as I approach the exit, something blocks it.

A dark green SUV.

I turn around, and the coffee shop guy is right there, on top of me. Before I can say anything or scream for help, a hand covers my mouth from behind. I'm having trouble breathing as my claustrophobia seizes me with dread even though my nose is uncovered and I can get plenty of air.

"Don't scream, Cassie. We won't hurt you. I promise. Just get in the car," a familiar voice says.

I don't believe him for a minute, so I try to bite his hand, but he's wearing gloves. Then they shuttle me into the back seat and slam the door shut. I can't see the driver in the front seat. I'm sandwiched between the two of them and I hear the doors lock.

I'm screwed.

FIFTEEN

Miles

"I've got some good news and some bad news," I say.

"What do you mean?" Brooke narrows her eyes at me as she sits with her legs crossed, tapping a pen on her notepad. We're in her office, sitting side by side in the two swivel chairs that face her desk.

She's not going to like this, so I decide to get right to the point. Rip off the Band-Aid, then go in with some palliative measures to try to ease her pain. I'm telling her at work, so she can't go too ballistic.

"The board isn't going for it, Brooke."

"The board isn't going for what?"

"You. As interim head."

"What the hell, Miles!" Her nostrils flare and her jaw tenses.

"I know, I know. It sucks. It's totally unfair. You've done so much for this place." I reach over and put my hand on her shoulder.

I've learned a bit about women over the years. I know I need to sympathize and validate her feelings before I try to "fix" the problem. I need to let her get the emotional wave of disappointment and anger out of her system first. I see some tears forming, and I take that as a good sign. Sadness is better than anger. Easier to contain.

"After everything that's happened, they feel it would be too…controversial. And maybe a little disrespectful. They don't like the optics."

She takes a deep breath. "This is all such a nightmare."

"Well, I said I had some good news too." I smile at her and at the realization that she's being quite reasonable. So far.

Maybe it will all work out.

But then I still haven't told her the worst part.

"What's your good news?"

"I found something else for you. An interim head of school position at a small day school outside Dallas. For next school year. Starting this summer."

"What do you mean you 'found something else' for me?"

"All you need to do is apply. There's no guarantee about a permanent job. You'll have to compete for that. But it's pretty much a done deal on the one-year appointment. The board and I are backing you on it. I've already talked to their board chair. They're not going internal, and they don't want to do an outside search for an interim appointment, so they reached out to our network. You can stay on and finish up the year here in your current role. Then you get your fresh start in the summer, and you'll have the inside track on the permanent position."

I can see her wheels turning. It's actually a good opportunity, and Brooke's not stupid. She'll see that this is all for the best.

"Of course, we'll help out with all your relocation expenses, and there's even a small severance package."

"It sounds like I'm being fired."

"We're not firing you. If you want to stay on as dean of faculty, it's your choice. But the head of school door is closed for you at Falcon Ridge. I strongly suggest you take this deal."

"And who's going to take over as interim head of school?"

I hesitate because I know this might push her over the edge. "Madeline," I say. "With my help. And with the help of Butch MacDonald."

"Your *wife?*" Her eyes look like they might pop out of her head.

"It wasn't my idea, Brooke. She's been a school administrator before. It was a while ago, but the board thinks in the short term, it will work. She doesn't want the job in the long term, so she'll cooperate fully with the permanent search. She's just a placeholder, which is what we need right now."

"A very convenient placeholder for you." Brooke sits there, silently steaming, and then she starts scribbling something on her notepad. She looks up at me when she's done. "Get me the application information. I'll take the deal. Now can you please leave? I have work to do."

As I stand, she holds up her notepad and lets me read it, and I'm thankful that her outburst is a silent one. The walls have ears around here.

This isn't over.

Meet me at our spot.

Tomorrow at 4.

Or I swear I'll ruin you.

———

I'm headed for my car, eager to get away from Falcon Ridge Academy, at least for today.

Well, that certainly could have gone better.

It wasn't my idea to install Madeline as interim head of school, but I could see how Brooke might get that idea. I'll explain it to her more when I see her in private. And I'm thankful she had the self-control to contain her emotional outbursts to her notepad, for now, because things could have gone worse too.

I would much rather have appointed Brooke as interim head of school. But the other board members expressed valid concerns, especially the incoming chair, who is scheduled to replace me in the fall. I couldn't make too much of a fuss without fueling more speculation. Although the board unwittingly presented me with a golden opportunity to fix one problem, especially if Madeline defers to me and simply acts as a figurehead, this arrangement is rife with potential pitfalls.

First, I don't want Madeline to know about the financial mess and the crime I may have committed, and now there's more of a chance she could find out. I can't let that happen because if she were somehow complicit in the cover-up, we'd both be in legal jeopardy. What would happen to Erin if they both went to prison?

There's no way I can allow Madeline to be a part of any kind of cover-up. I'll come clean and accept the consequences if she catches wind of it. But she won't. Not if I can close this donor and eliminate the need for a loan. I'm getting close, but nothing much will happen over the holidays. And because of that, it promises to be a tense rather than a relaxing week off, which is exactly what I don't need.

Nothing's going to happen this week with my development project either. Everyone's enjoying their holiday, everyone except for us. Madeline officially starts her new position after the new year. But we'll need to pop in and take care of some of the more pressing issues, so we'll both be working a bit at the school.

At least Brooke is taking some time off, so I'll get a break from her. We had to cancel our family trip to Aruba, much to my disappointment. I was looking forward to a week away from this place, and a chance to reconnect with my family. We settled for a few nights in Manhattan at the Plaza, starting the day after next.

This leaves me tomorrow to meet with Brooke and try to get her under control. Then maybe I can enjoy a few nights off. I haven't been sleeping well, and the strain is getting to me. My head feels heavy, as if I have a hangover, although I haven't touched a drop of alcohol in over a week. Last night was particularly bad. I fell asleep pretty quickly, but I didn't stay asleep. I woke up after a few hours, trying in vain to fall back asleep while a host of horrific scenarios played out in my mind. When I finally drifted off, I had a terrible nightmare. It was vivid when I woke up this morning, but now the details have mostly faded.

Except for one image that's forever burned into my mind's eye.

My wife's dead body, lying at the bottom of the stairs at the Cortlandt train station.

SIXTEEN

Cassie

A split second after the doors lock, before I even have time to panic, the two of them turn to me as I sit wedged between them, flash their badges at me, and utter two words, almost in unison.

"Federal agents."

Then they simultaneously lower their hands. In an instant, everything makes sense.

"Let me see those again." I take a closer look at their badges. The coffee shop guy is a federal marshal, and Dan Moralis is FBI.

"Where are you taking me? Am I under arrest?"

"We'll explain later, Cassie," Dan says.

"I asked you if I'm under arrest. I have a right to know."

"Please, Ms. Romano. We'll explain everything when we get to the station," coffee shop guy replies.

I suppose I should be skeptical, given the way they went about this, but my gut is telling me they're for real. I don't think they're kidnapping me, but I'm sure I'm in some kind of trouble. They probably know that I broke into Dan's room.

If he's FBI, I've got this all wrong. He's not Brooke's plant. He's some sort of undercover agent.

But what is he trying to uncover?

And do they think I have something to do with it?

I'm sitting in a dank, featureless room with no windows, nothing to distract me, and it's making my palms sweat and my heart race. The lights above me are bright and intimidating as I step near the table and into their wash, and I'm trying not to think about whether the door is locked and if I'm actually trapped in here against my will.

Breathe.

We're at the local police station. A female officer is with me but hasn't said anything. I want to ask questions, but I know that the best thing to do in a situation like this is to keep my mouth shut and lawyer up. My father taught me that too.

She finally speaks. "Do you want anything to drink?" she asks.

I don't, but even if I did, I wouldn't take it. That's how they get your DNA. Plus, I don't want to have to pee. *Would they even let me?*

"No thanks."

After a while, Dan and the coffee shop guy come into the room, and the female officer excuses herself.

"I'm Cory Wilson," the marshal says. "I'm with WITSEC. We know who you are, and we brought you in like this to protect your identity."

"You almost gave me a heart attack. But thanks."

I can see Dan fight to suppress a smile. And then it hits me. Dan knows who I really am.

How long has he known?

"We're the only ones who know, Cassie, and we're planning to keep it that way. Local law enforcement doesn't need to know. That isn't what this is about," Dan says. "We just want to ask you a few questions."

"I want a lawyer."

But I can't afford a lawyer, and I'm not sure if I can get a public defender if I'm not under arrest. But I do know I can refuse to answer their questions.

"You're not under arrest."

"It certainly feels like I am. And I'm not answering any of your questions without a lawyer. So, you can either arrest me and get me a lawyer, or you can let me go."

"Let's try this another way," Dan says. "I'll talk, and you can just listen. How does that sound?"

I roll my eyes. "Sure." *What choice do I have?*

"We know you broke into my room, and we know you're planning to leave town. Don't try to deny it, because we know. But what we don't know is why." He pauses, waiting for some sort of response, but I'm not that stupid.

"We're also pretty sure you're the one who sent Kimi Choy's letter to the police station."

I take a deep breath. I'm sure he's expecting me to say *what letter?* But I don't. If I deny it, that will only hurt me later if they have some way of proving it. So I say nothing. As I said, I've had a lot of practice staying cool under pressure, and I have a good poker face. They both look as if they could wait all day. Probably a tactic of theirs. I don't budge either. After a while, he continues.

"Kimi obviously trusted you, and I know you were in her room that day ostensibly to pack up for her. But I'm guessing, based on the fact that you were carrying pepper spray that you subsequently used on me, that you have your suspicions about her death. So, my logical conclusion is that you didn't believe me that I went in there to get the book. And you broke into my room to check up on me. You wanted to make sure I wasn't somehow complicit in her death, which is why we aren't planning to press charges for the break-in. At least right now. But we could. Anytime."

"What do you want from me?"

"We want your cooperation. We want your…assistance."

"I told you. I'm not answering any questions without a lawyer."

"I understand if you don't trust us, Cassie. But maybe there's someone else who can convince you that we're on your side."

"I doubt it."

"It's worth a try."

Dan nods to marshal man, who heads over to the door and opens it.

The marshal waves to someone outside and then steps aside to make room for the person to enter. I grab Dan's arm and let out a gasp and my heart literally skips a beat when I see who's standing in the doorway.

"Hi, Cassie," he says as he enters the room, pulls out a chair, and sits down while my mind races to process what's happening.

Doug Walker's alive?

PART TWO

Stay

SEVENTEEN

Cassie

So much has happened in the last week and a half, I've hardly been able to catch my breath. It's my first day back at work, a full schedule of faculty and staff meetings before classes begin tomorrow, and the first day of my new "assignment."

When Doug Walker strolled into the interrogation room that day, it took me a few minutes to get my bearings, but by the time they started to explain what was going on, I'd already figured some of it out, but not all of it.

"I bet you're surprised to see me," he said.

"You could say that." I still wasn't giving anything up without a lawyer though, so I let them do most of the talking.

First, they confirmed what I'd already figured out. They were faking Walker's death because what happened to him was somehow due to foul play, and pretending he was dead would give them a better chance of catching whoever was behind it.

Then Dan went on to explain that Falcon Ridge Academy has been under investigation as part of a federal effort to root out dirty money donations to educational institutions, something I would never have guessed. Apparently, it's a worrisome trend that's becoming more prevalent, especially for schools that take foreign students.

Independent schools and private universities strapped for cash are being used to launder money for increasingly problematic donors. One donor in particular put the school on their radar. But when they started to dig further into it, they noticed other financial irregularities at the school. They didn't expand on what they were.

"What does any of this have to do with me?" I asked.

"We think Kimi Choy was murdered because she found out something she shouldn't have."

"I see."

My wheels were turning. Kimi said in her letter that she was concerned about Brooke Baxter plotting something against Doug Walker.

Do they think Brooke had something to do with it? And do they think she did something to Kimi?

I had a hard time believing this at the time, and I still don't really buy it. She's a bad boss, but thinking of her as a murderer is a stretch for me. But maybe she told someone her suspicions about Kimi—someone more dangerous, like a person with dirty money to launder. But I still felt they might be considering me as a suspect—maybe they think money laundering runs in my family—so I didn't express any of these thoughts to them.

"You were brought in to investigate all of this?" I said to Dan.

He explained that when Kimi was found dead under suspicious circumstances, the opportunity to insert an undercover agent presented itself, and he was selected.

"So, you're not really an English teacher from an international school in Guatemala?" I asked. "That explains a lot."

"That part was true if you must know. I was teaching EFL though, not AP English, as my cover on that assignment. And I minored in English lit, by the way. We figured I could pull it off."

"EFL isn't AP English."

"I know that *now*, Cassie." He rolled his eyes at me.

I knew I was being a bit of an asshole, but he deserved it. And they still weren't getting to the point, and I was running out of patience.

"So, again, what does any of this have to do with me?"

"That's a fair question," Doug Walker chimed in. "We were hoping that, since you were friends with Kimi, you might be willing to help us out."

"Help you...how?"

Dan took over. "We're hoping you'll reconsider your decision to leave. That you'll stay on as English department chair."

"Why?"

Then Dan let out a long sigh and threw up his hands. "Because I'm not a very good English teacher."

"I'm sorry but...what?" At first, I thought it was a joke or another one of their tactics. But Dan looked serious.

"Cassie, you practically made me already. We've been working for years on this operation. I can't have my cover blown."

I had to fight not to crack up because it struck me as hilarious. But he seemed really broken up about it, and I needed him on my side, so I fought back my chuckle.

"You want me to stay on and..."

"Help me. These freaking kids are smart, Cassie. It's only the first week, and I'm already in over my head."

"So, let me get this straight. You want me to stay on at school and help you become a better English teacher so you don't blow your cover?"

"Yes. Exactly. And to keep Brooke Baxter off my case. She can't suspect anything. Nobody at the school knows, except you. And Doug, of course. And a few people on the board."

"So, you think Brooke had something to do with this?"

"We can't comment on that," Dan replied.

"What's in it for me?"

"The break-in goes away," Dan said. "We don't press charges."

"I'm going to need more than that. I'll just say I thought you were up to something, so I broke in and found a gun in your room. I could blow your cover."

"You won't. And I won't blow yours."

I noticed the marshal's eyes widen.

"Is that a threat?" I started to stand up like I was going to bolt, but then Dan walked it back.

"No. Not at all. That's not what I meant. I just meant that we'd have each other's backs at school, that's all. We wouldn't have to pretend. At least not in front of each other."

I was skeptical about his sudden change of tune. Dan was obviously desperate to stay on this case and close it, and it seemed he'd do whatever he needed to do to make that happen. And even if he didn't mean it the way he said it, they clearly had me where they wanted me. I was an easy mark, with my father's checkered past and my breaking and entering transgression.

Then Doug Walker stepped in to try and mollify me. "Give us your terms, Cassie, and we'll see what we can do. We're pretty pressed for time. I can't stay dead forever. We've got a limited window of time to pull this off. We need to wrap this up in a few weeks. That's all we're asking of you."

"How are you planning to wrap this up in a few weeks?"

"We can't tell you that, Cassie. It's a need-to-know situation. Just know that you won't be in any danger. The operation itself has nothing to do with you, so you don't need to know about it," Dan replied.

A pained look washed over Doug's face. "Do it for Kimi. Please. She's the real victim here. And that's partly my fault."

"What do you mean, your fault? How?"

Doug took a deep breath, then he continued. "Kimi and I knew each other from years ago. We worked at the same school, but I asked her to keep that under wraps. I had a feeling Brooke was up to something. I knew she was milking Kimi for information—trying to find out who on the faculty was against her—and that Brooke had it in for me. I asked her to keep an ear out, that's all. Tell me if she heard anything unusual. I had no idea something of a dangerous nature was happening at the school. In my wildest dreams I wouldn't have thought that—"

"Doug? I don't like where this is headed." Dan looked over at Doug, but he didn't tell him to stop. "Tread carefully."

Doug gave him a dismissive wave of his hand and continued. "She called me that morning. Said she had some information for me. And judging from the time of the phone call, it was only a few minutes before she was killed. Whatever Brooke's mixed up in, it's a lot more complicated than petty jealousy over a promotion. And that phone call to me may have gotten her killed. Someone might have heard it. I don't know who, but—"

"Doug?" Dan put his hand on Doug's shoulder. "That's enough for now." He turned to me. "We've already told you more than you need to know. Are you in? Will you help us?"

At that point, I turned to the marshal, whose name continued to escape me. The one who was supposed to be on my side. The one whose job it is to protect me.

"I want to talk to my parents and my handler. And I want an attorney before we go any further with this."

The truth was, they didn't really need to talk me into staying, but I wasn't going to let them know that. I was overcome with a sudden desire to stay on and help, and this caught me totally by surprise. I wasn't quite aware of what was behind my sudden change of heart. Partly, I'm sure, it was for Kimi, to stay and see justice served, especially now that my hunch was confirmed, and to ease the guilt I felt about abandoning our friendship. If I stayed, I could continue my behind-the-scenes detective work on her behalf.

It was also a way to atone for the sins of my father, to make it clear that I am on the right side of the law. Plus, I've always loved a good mystery. And the idea of being at the center of a real-life one gave me a thrill I've never experienced before. If I'm being honest, it also didn't hurt that Dan would be living next door, and now he knew who I really was.

The thought of having someone—anyone—in my life who knew my secret was too tempting to pass up, and not just because he's a hunk. Even if he turned out to be only a friend or an acquaintance, the thought of being able to be myself, of being able to be open about who I am, seemed worth the minor risk I'd be taking. I wondered how much of his career had been spent undercover. Maybe, like me, he was hungry to have someone around who knew the truth about him, to be able to be himself. Even for a short part of the day.

To make a long story short, they met all my conditions, and I agreed to stay on. I told them they'd have to pay my tutoring fee—a hundred dollars an hour—for anything above and beyond the normal time I'd spend with a teacher as department chair. They agreed.

The attorney my parents hired assured me that the document they drew up and had me sign was solid. Nothing would come of my breaking and entering, and if I felt I was in danger at any point, I could leave. I had that in writing. All they asked was that I give it a try.

Since the odds of my getting a job before next school year were slim to none, I figured this was also the practical career move. I'd even have a semester of administrative experience under my belt to add to my resume. Besides, my decision to leave had been based more on loneliness and boredom than anything else. I wasn't really afraid for my life then, and I'm not now.

"I'll be right next door, making sure you're safe," Dan assured me.

I'd like to think I'm the kind of gal who can take care of herself, not the kind who needs a knight in shining armor. But the thought of having one right next door made me go a little weak in the knees, in spite of the fact that he's basically blackmailing me. Hopefully, he's better at slaying dragons than he is at teaching English.

I'm not taking any chances though, and I still keep my pepper spray with me at all times. I can feel it in my pants pocket right now as I make my way to our first faculty-staff meeting after a too-short winter break. Classes start tomorrow, and we have a lot to do.

They've appointed Madeline Kensington, the board chair's wife, as interim head of school, and I'm assuming she'll be addressing us today, along with Brooke. It feels a bit out of left field to me. She seemed more like the professional soccer mom type when I met with her that one time, when I was concerned about her daughter Erin and her weak essay. But she had some kind of principal position a while back, so I guess it's not too much of a stretch. I bet Brooke's steaming about it, though.

This should be interesting.

EIGHTEEN

Madeline

"You look great. Ready for your big day?" Miles says this from the driver's seat of our Lexus as we start up the mountain road to Falcon Ridge for my first official day on the job.

"Of course," I reply.

More than you know.

I almost feel bad for Miles when I see the way he looks at me like I'm some sort of holy relic up on a pedestal.

Almost.

But I don't. Because it's all his fault.

If he hadn't slept with Brooke Baxter, I wouldn't have had to go this far. The financial mess he got us into I could have lived with, even though I told him not to start on that office project. But the betrayal? He needs to pay for that, and so does the shrew.

I'm not a monster, and I do feel bad about that teacher, but then she should have minded her own business. I saw her that day outside the door to Brooke's office, standing there listening to their conversation, but I couldn't hear much myself. I had a hunch it was something important though, and when I listened to the recordings from my husband's study that night, I almost blew a gasket. It took everything I had not to go up to our bedroom, grab Miles, and shake him awake.

How could they be so stupid, to talk about it at school?

That's why I had to bug his study in the first place. He does stupid things, and I need to know what I'm dealing with so I can get ahead of it and keep us on track. I'd do anything to preserve what we have and to make sure Erin's life is financially stable, unlike my own.

I was impulsive, I'll admit that. I think it was my hormones that week. At first, I was only planning to go over to campus and follow that Choy woman to see if she was simply going to leave town like a good girl or if she was going to tell someone about their idiotic plan to bring down Doug Walker.

Deepfake videos?

Give me a break. They were laughable, and luckily, I caught wind of their ridiculous plan and blocked them before they were sent out and made things even worse for us. Like I said, my husband does stupid things. But I made sure to plant them on Brooke's hard drive, in a place she's unlikely to look.

When I saw Kimi Choy leave a letter for Brooke that Friday afternoon, I grabbed it, snuck into the ladies' room, read it, and put it back in her box. I was beyond thrilled. I thought maybe we were in luck. She seemed to be running scared. Quitting. Leaving town and never coming back.

But I wasn't taking it for granted, and I decided to see her off. So, I went to the school at the crack of dawn that morning and waited. When I saw her loading her bags into an Uber, I figured our little problem might take care of itself. But an opportunity presented itself to take care of two problems, so I followed her, prepared to do what I needed to do to make sure my interests were protected. And it's a good thing I did, because right before she went into the train station, she hesitated. Then she called someone and left a message. Said she had some "important information" and that the person should contact her right away.

I did what I had to do.

What choice did I have?

And Doug Walker? He must have been in worse shape than I thought. I didn't mean to kill him. I only gave him enough Digoxin to cause a moderate cardiac event. I thought it would get him to take some time off and free up the head of school job, because getting him out of the way was the only good idea Miles had. Except there was no way I was going to let Brooke Baxter take his place. My husband thinks it was the board's idea to have me step in.

Think again, Miles.

No, I don't want the job. I just want to fix this mess and get on with my life. I'm perfectly happy being a stay-at-home mom. I see these ambitious career women trying to "have it all." I'm sure they all had nice mommies and daddies who gave them ballet lessons and math tutors and lots of love and encouragement. I'm sure none of them worked at a greasy diner from the age of fourteen, scalding their hands on burning hot plates while their fat slob boss snuck in ass pinches.

I was perfectly content to marry Miles and let him do all the heavy lifting, especially after Erin was born. I wanted to give her everything I never had, including a doting, stay-at-home mom who volunteered at school and served on committees and watched her back. But then I realized that my husband's not that smart. And disappointingly lacking in ambition.

In the beginning, he impressed me with his family connections and country club lifestyle. I was naive. I knew nothing about high society, and the Kensingtons had some social clout in Albany, where they're from, but I soon realized that's worth nothing in Manhattan. I've been pushing him for years to use his connections to make some inroads where it really matters. To take us to the next level, socially and financially.

I thought we'd be somewhere else by now, like Park Avenue or Scarsdale, but we're not. We're in Marlboro, "one of the nicest hamlets in Ulster County," as my husband's pointed out to me on numerous occasions when I've tried to nudge us farther south. He's content to be a big fish in a small pond, so here I am, circling around in the muck, trying to clean up his mess.

I realize now that I jumped the gun on the husband thing. I was young when I met him, working my way through college. If I'd waited a bit longer, I could have attracted someone more formidable. Men have always fawned over me. I just needed some more time to refine myself so I could attract the right ones.

Live and learn.

But he dazzled me, and I must admit, we were happy for many years. I've had lots of opportunities to stray, with men much richer and more powerful than my husband. But I made a vow. Unlike my husband, I've stayed true to it, and I'm not letting him and his little tart ruin us. I won't let my daughter be subjected to the stress and humiliation of poverty. If he goes down, he's not taking us with him, although I'll do what I can to keep him out of prison. What could I possibly gain from that? I have a better plan to pay back my husband for the betrayal. But one step at a time.

For now, I'll play dumb and do the job. I'll let Miles and Butch MacDonald "help" me through the tricky parts. I'll let my husband think he found the miracle donor that saved us. And then I'll make my move on him.

But Brooke Baxter?

She's going down for murder.

Soon.

NINETEEN

Miles

I haven't been looking forward to this day. In fact, I've been dreading it. For the last week or so, I was able to pretend that everything was fine. Our family getaway in the city was a little slice of heaven. For a few days I was able to block out all the stress and enjoy life. And Brooke was away last week, so when Madeline and I worked together at the school, it felt pretty comfortable.

Butch MacDonald, the former head of school, agreed to coach Madeline through some of the procedural parts of the job, and thankfully, the board went for it. Because Butch has as much reason to make sure our financial dealings stay buried as I do. My plan seems solid, all except for Brooke, the wild card.

There's a lot riding on this week, including a meeting with the donor who has the potential to make this all go away. With Doug Walker out of the picture, the situation is less urgent because he was the one pushing the hardest for a loan. Some other board members were on Doug's side, and I don't want people to get suspicious if I try to steer them away from it, so I've said nothing against it and instead have been working on securing the donation.

Then there's the impending clash of Madeline and Brooke. There's bound to be some bad blood there, on Brooke's part, but I'm hoping I can contain it. Madeline had been acting a little distant the last month or so, and for a while, I thought she might suspect something. But she seems to be warming back up to me—even in the carnal sense—so I figure I'm in the clear.

I have a hard time thinking she'd believe the rumors, even if she heard them. I've never given her a reason to think I would stray. I'm home with her nearly every evening by dinnertime. I always pick up her calls. I'm hopelessly taken with her and have been since the day I laid eyes on her. She has a hold over me that no other woman could possibly challenge. Hopefully, she knows that.

When I met with Brooke at our usual spot, after that meeting in her office with the minor outburst which she kept contained to her notepad, she had some further demands.

Monetary demands.

She demanded another hundred grand to go away, on top of the severance package the board was offering. And she wanted it from me.

Or else.

I brushed her off at first and explained to her, once again, that she had no leverage. She was complicit in the scandal too, and I had the paper trail with the payouts to prove it. If she came forward, she'd go down too. Even if the authorities were more lenient with her, I reasoned, it would ruin her career. Her life.

And then she came out with a threat that nearly blew my mind.

"I'm not planning to come forward about the financial shenanigans, Miles. I'm planning to sue you for sexual harassment."

"What? Are you *insane*? We haven't even had sex! I've never once so much as touched you."

"But everybody thinks we have."

That much is true.

At first, we met at the motel just outside of town because there was no other good spot to meet to discuss our plans, and it would be too risky if we were seen in public, at a café or restaurant. It was Brooke's suggestion, and initially, I was concerned she had gotten the wrong idea. She'd always been a little flirty around me, and if I'm being honest, I probably took advantage of that to get her to conceal my financial irregularities and go along with my idea.

But her flirty behavior died down over time, and the arrangement became strictly business, at least to me. About two months ago, someone saw us at the motel—I'm still not sure who—and rumors started to circulate. Rather than quashing them, I let them percolate because having an affair isn't a crime. Any other plausible explanation for our meetups could land me in prison. And that's why I can't tell Madeline the truth. If I told her the real reason I was meeting with Brooke all the time, she would be an accessory to my crime. And I couldn't take that risk.

"Brooke, what the fuck? How could you do this to me?"

"How could I do what to you? *You* did this to *me*, Miles. You screwed up my entire life. You used me to fix your financial mess. You flirted with me. You led me on. And then you dangled the job in front of me, pretending you were a bigger wig than you are. And then you gave *my* job to your wife."

"Brooke. Please. Don't do this. That wasn't my idea. I swear."

Up until that point, I hadn't considered the possibility that Brooke might actually have developed feelings for me. But that would explain a lot. And it would also make her a great deal more dangerous. Love made rational people do irrational things. Was Brooke in love with me? It would certainly explain why she vacillates between anger and forgiveness. But there's a fine line between love and hate, and if she's crossed it, there's no telling what she might do.

"Oh, and then you accused me of murder."

"I did not—"

"I don't trust you for a nanosecond, Miles. I'm getting what I need out of this. And you're not getting away from this unscathed. You've got two weeks to get me the money. Or I sue."

"Brooke. I swear, I never meant to hurt you."

"Shut up, Miles. You're making it worse. Two weeks, or you're screwed."

That's the last time I had any contact with her, and my time is almost up. I have no idea where her head's at today. I drive into the parking lot at Falcon Ridge, pull the car into the head of school's space, and take a deep breath. Then I look over at my wife.

"You want to go over your speech one more time?"

"No, Miles. Don't worry. I've got this."

Then she leans over and gives me a long, lingering kiss. When we come up for air, I brush the hair back from her face, once again enchanted by my wife. She's so unpredictable, and I find that intoxicating.

"What was that for?"

"Can't a wife kiss her husband?" She's got that sly, sexy smile on her face, the one that drives me insane with desire.

But we have to get going, so I need to get a handle on my raging libido. Still, when I open the car door, there's a big grin spreading across my face, until I see Brooke standing near the entrance of the administration building, looking at us with daggers in her eyes before the corners of her mouth lift a bit, concealing her wrath.

"Welcome back, you two. Happy New Year," she calls out with a forced smile that's at odds with her tense jaw. Then she turns from us and walks through the doorway.

Shit.

———

The morning ended on a much better note, thankfully. Once we got inside, everything seemed fine, and I started to think I was letting my paranoia get the best of me. That I'd possibly imagined the scorned look on Brooke's face. The stress was obviously getting to me, and I needed to find a better way to deal with it.

Because Madeline and Brooke were not only professional in their first official business meeting, they were downright friendly. It was a short meeting, but it set things on the right course. It was held in the head of school's office—Madeline's new workspace—and although it's one of the larger offices at the school, that's not saying much. It's functional but on the smaller side for a position of that level and badly in need of renovation.

The work area houses a large walnut desk that takes up too much space, a few bookshelves, a large filing cabinet, and two leather swivel chairs facing the massive desk. As a consequence, the sitting area is a bit cramped. A compact brown leather loveseat butts up against the wall near the small closet, with a club chair kitty-corner to it. It made me nervous that Brooke and Madeline would be in such close proximity.

When my wife sat in the club chair, I was forced to sit next to Brooke on the loveseat. I positioned myself on the far side, so the two women would be facing each other and I'd have a good vantage point from which to observe their interaction. They were so close together, their knees almost touched, and if I didn't know better, I'd have thought they were good friends. They went over the order of events for the faculty-staff meeting, and Madeline thanked Brooke for her support. I'm confident now that Madeline doesn't suspect anything.

The larger meeting went very well too. I started it off and then gave the floor to Brooke. Brooke introduced Madeline. We'd all agreed it would be better that way, rather than having her husband do it. Her address was short and to the point, with just the right touch of authority and humility. I felt proud.

Then Madeline informed everyone about the celebration of life at the school for Doug Walker. His family had held a small, private ceremony in Atlanta, where he was from, over Christmas break. His wife and kids had stayed there to finish out the school year, so they had no real connection to Falcon Ridge. But everyone at school needed some closure, so we decided we'd organize a celebration for him. During her talk, it crossed my mind that we should probably include that teacher too, and I made a mental note to point that out to Brooke, Madeline, and the other board members. And then it wrapped up without further incident.

Now, I'm trying to figure out how to get a message to Brooke that I'll have her money in a few days, a method that won't leave any evidence. Then I need to get going to my donor meeting. I took out an equity line of credit on one of my properties—one of the few in my portfolio that didn't need Madeline's approval—to get the hundred grand for Brooke, but that is about all I can access, and I'm starting to worry that she might never be satisfied.

What if she continues to blackmail me forever?

At some point, I'd have to say no and take my chances on the lawsuit. It's he-said, she-said as far as the sexual harassment, so I'd let it run its course. Hopefully, she takes the head of school job at the other school, along with my payoff, and gets on with her life.

I turn the corner and almost run smack into her.

"Hi, Brooke. Nice job this morning."

"Thanks, Miles." Her expression is neutral, and I can't quite get a read on her.

"I've got that…information you wanted."

"Great. Can we meet tomorrow, around five?"

"Works for me."

I exit the administration building and head for my car to go close the deal I've been working on, and then I can finally breathe easier. *Five million dollars.* It's a big ask. If we get it, it will be the largest single donation in the school's history.

I've never actually met the donor. Whoever it is works through a representative of his, or her, foundation. It seemed a little sketchy at first, but Butch MacDonald assured me it was all aboveboard and that it's quite common these days, for donors to keep their identities private, especially for schools that take foreign donations. This is an international foundation with a mission to help refugees from war-torn countries. They're supposedly impressed by the fact that Falcon Ridge gives scholarships to refugee students.

I took Butch at his word and didn't investigate any further. Even if it's not totally aboveboard, I'm in no position to look a gift horse in the mouth, so I'll keep my concerns to myself, take the money, and move on with my life. I don't need to go looking for problems.

TWENTY

Cassie

"I think that's enough for one day."

My neck is cramping up, and Dan's eyes are glazing over. I let out a long sigh, then I stretch my neck from side to side. We're in Dan's room, huddled at his desk. We've been at this for over two hours now, trying to get him ready for his classes, which start tomorrow. We decided to go one week at a time, and even that's seeming a bit ambitious now. There's so much ground to cover.

He nods and sits up straight, then arches his back. "I could use a break."

"You feel okay about the next few days of classes?"

"Yeah. I'm good. I'll be fine. Thanks."

He's actually pretty solid on the literary themes. But he needs help on how to deliver the material to high school students, how to make it interesting for them, what kind of questions to ask, how to keep the discussions going when they start to peter out, and how to teach the skills for the AP test. There's also a lot of tech stuff to master. The students expect course information to be accessible online, so we've spent a fair amount of time on the course management system.

And this has to be the most mind-numbingly boring undercover assignment in the history of the profession. I'm dying to find out what's really going on. Who they suspect is behind this. Whether Brooke is on their radar. But I'm waiting for the right time. I'm not sure I'll get anything out of him. But I'm going to try.

"I need to stand up and move around," I say.

Dan's face lights up. "Hey, I have an idea. Why don't I help you brush up on your self-defense moves? Sort of like a quid pro quo."

"It's not a quid pro quo if I'm being paid."

"Well, consider it part of your training then. As an operative."

"I got away from you, didn't I?" I flash him a wry smile, but I shouldn't be so smug. I really could use some training. It's not a bad idea.

"Lucky break, Romano."

"Right."

"Seriously, you were pretty good with the pepper spray, but then, you saw me coming. Did someone teach you that evasive move?"

"Yeah. My dad. You duck and shift to the side of the attacker after you blind them, 'cause their instinct is to lunge forward at you. And then you get away as fast as you can while the attacker is still blinded and confused."

"But it'd be totally different if they caught you by surprise. You'd have a good chance of not getting your hand up in time or of missing their eyes altogether and just pissing them off more."

"I know, I know. I could use some training. You're right."

"Then let's get to it."

We stand, and he's obviously eager to be in his element. It has to be a bit of a blow to his ego, the way I'm coaching him through the most basic teaching tasks, even if he's only pretending to be an English teacher. I can tell he feels good about being in the expert role now.

"Okay. We'll start with two of the most common ways someone can grab you. The arm grab and coming up from behind."

"Whatever you say."

Then I realize this might get quite intimate. I feel a flutter of excitement, and my face starts to flush. I think about how it will feel to have his body so close to mine. I'm getting better at keeping the pheromone rush contained when I'm around him, but we haven't had any physical contact yet. I tell myself to get a grip, that it's ridiculous to even go there. Not to mention inappropriate. But my body has a mind of its own, and I can't fight my own biology. *But what about him? Does he feel any attraction to me at all?*

First, he pulls up a video of a man training a woman and shows me the two moves we'll be working on. The first one is pretty tame in terms of contact. The attacker simply grabs an arm, and the woman breaks his grip. But the second one has a lot more body contact. The man grabs the woman from behind. Just thinking about him doing that to me sets off a flurry of tingles that threatens to unnerve me to the point where I won't be able to think straight. It's also a hard move to pull off, and I don't want to make an idiot of myself.

We try the arm move, and the first few times I can't shake him.

"You've got to point your elbow higher to get the leverage, or it won't work. Then twist it down into your core, and let your core strength do the work." He plays the video again, at a slower speed.

"Let me try again."

This time, I break his grip, but he won't let me move on. We do it again. He grips me, harder this time. So hard that

I'm afraid I might have a faint bruise where his hand was. I don't get it on the first try, but I do on the second one.

I rub my arm.

"You okay?"

"Sure."

"You want me to go easier on you?"

"No. I'm not planning to go easy on you."

I get a smirk out of him.

"But I don't want to have to explain a bruise on my arm."

"Good point. Let's try the second move. Then we can call it a day. I'm hungry."

"Okay. Me too."

"So, with this move, I'm coming at you from behind. I'm going to grab you. Like this."

He puts his entire body on mine and wraps it around me. It's firm and warm as his arms encircle me and hold me tight, like a bear hug. Evan was a lot thinner. Dan is so much more substantial, and the security I feel with his bulk up against me is titillating. That and the faint scent of his body wash sends shock waves through me, and I think about how long it's been since I've had sex.

Too long.

I wonder if it's been a while for him too. With all the undercover work, there's not likely to be too much time for romance. He lingers a bit longer than necessary, and then he releases me. I take a deep breath and try to compose myself, then slowly turn around. By this time, he's at the computer.

"Now watch what you need to do." He taps his finger on the computer screen while I try to stop thinking about sex and what it would be like to have him on top of me. "Watch her."

I force myself to focus. I see the woman in the video lean all her weight forward, punch him in the groin, shift to the side, and swing her leg back around to knee him in the nuts. It's a hard move to pull off because she has to twist far enough over to get leverage and then deliver the hit from a weird angle.

"Okay. Let's try it. Turn around," he says as he puts his hands on my shoulders and guides me. "And I'm not coming right away. We need an element of surprise. So be patient."

It's a tense standoff, with him behind me, not knowing when he's going to grab me, and it's actually making me nervous, but not in a sexy way. I picture myself walking in the alley with coffee shop guy behind me to draw on that fear I felt, and it's working. My heart starts to race.

Then suddenly he grabs me, and I feel a surge of adrenaline, but I can't break his grip. I wriggle around, but I can't shift to the side like the woman in the video. After a bit, he releases me, but not before I experience what it would feel like to be in that position for real.

I let out a sigh.

"It's okay. It's hard. You have to remember to lean forward and push back on me with all your weight first, then swing your fist into my nuts so I pull back more and give you the space to turn, or it won't work."

"Right."

We try the move a few more times, and I'm getting better, but I'm not really putting my all into it. I'm worried I might knee him in the groin too forcefully when I swing around. He assures me he can protect himself. He's a pro, so I make myself get over it and go for it, but I still can't twist around enough to pull it off.

"One more time," he says. "Then we'll call it a day."

This time, I'm able to twist around and get my knee up, but I stop short of slamming it into him. I could though if I had to.

"Better! Now let's go eat."

We wrap up and head to the front door. When he opens it he places his hand on the small of my back and gently ushers me out. Then a thought pops into my head. *I'm not his boss anymore.* Not really. We're coworkers. An undercover team. And there'd be nothing wrong with a meaningless fling. I wonder if that's occurred to him too.

———

We get in line at the cafeteria, and I see Ed about ten spots ahead of us. People will probably start talking if they see Dan and me together too much. I know I'm not really his boss, but nobody else does, so we need to be careful. On the other hand, Dan and I live on the same floor, so I suppose it's not unreasonable that we'd run into each other a lot.

After we fill our plates, we join Ed at his table.

"I heard they're planning to add Kimi to the celebration of life service," Ed says.

"Good," I say. "They should. It's totally awkward that they failed to include her in the first place."

Especially since she's the one who's actually dead.

And that brings me back to reality and the reason I'm staying here in the first place. Finding Kimi's killer. Dan excuses himself to go to the restroom, leaving me alone with Ed. We haven't been alone together in a while.

"How was the visit with your parents?"

I tell him that it was great. Because it was. I felt, for the first time in ages, like my relationship with my father was getting back on course. Maybe it's because I'm growing up, or maybe it's because I experienced being interrogated, accused of something, and misunderstood.

I realize now that I should have given my father the benefit of the doubt. If he says he didn't know the goods were stolen, maybe he didn't. Although in truth, I have a hard time believing it. I feel like there was too much remorse for him to have been totally innocent. Perhaps he suspected but didn't really know, and simply turned a blind eye. But I am starting to forgive him, and it's helping me heal too. Mom was concerned about my staying to help with the investigation and tried to talk me out of it, but Dad understood immediately why I needed to do it.

"You and Dan seem to be getting pretty chummy."

"I'm helping him with AP. He's never taught it before."

"If that's what you kids are calling it these days."

"What? *No.* I'm his supervisor, Ed." I feel my face flush for the second time today.

"Oh my God. You're blushing. Nobody cares about that, Cassie. Who else are you going to meet, stuck up here on this mountain? Everyone does it. How do you think I met my wife? I see the way he looks at you. Go for it."

"The way he looks at me?"

"You haven't noticed?"

"No. Not really."

"That ex of yours really did a number on you. I know a bit about guys, Cassie. I am one, after all. And he's into you."

Dan comes back to the table, and we all eat in silence for a bit. I look over at Ed, and he winks at me. I widen my eyes and press my lips together to suppress my smile, with the sensation of Dan's body wrapped around mine still fresh in my mind. Dan's oblivious, busy chowing down his burger.

Then I think about what Ed said. I glance around the cafeteria and wonder who else is hooking up to get through the long, cold winter ahead.

TWENTY-ONE

Miles

I'm in the living room when my wife and daughter arrive home from the first day of second semester. And I'm in a terrific mood because I actually did it. I closed the deal. I felt pretty good yesterday after the meeting, but the donor's representative said he needed a day to discuss it with the donor. An hour ago, I got the confirmation call.

Five million dollars.

There's no need for a loan now. Which means no audit. No discovery of my padded invoices. That nightmare is over, and I can finally get on with my life. Whatever I was guilty of, it can't be anything worse than embezzlement. I checked, and the statute of limitations on that is two to five years, so I'm pretty confident this donation will keep me out of prison. There should be no need to look back at the school's finances, at least not for a while. Not with that kind of money coming in. As long as Brooke keeps her mouth shut, I should be in the clear.

"Hey, my two favorite ladies. How was the first day of classes?"

I'm anxious to tell my wife about the donation. I don't want to steal her thunder, though. Even though her position is temporary, it's a pretty big honor to be given that level of responsibility. I'm hoping it will motivate her to do something afterwards. That maybe it will whet her appetite for more. Being a stay-at-home mom of a nearly college-age child doesn't seem like much of a life. The truth is, I'd find her more interesting if she had something else going on. Before she took the head of school job, she spent a lot of time at Falcon Ridge volunteering, but I can't see her doing that after Erin graduates. I wonder what she'll do with herself all day.

I realize that, although it never got physical with Brooke, I enjoyed the intellectual stimulation I received from our encounters. She's sharp and innovative and cute. Perhaps I did use her and lead her on in a way, although I wasn't conscious of it. She has a right to be upset with me, and I told her so this afternoon. Thankfully, she seemed content with taking the hundred grand and the new job and moving on with her life this summer.

"Fine," Madeline says. "Routine."

Routine is good.

"Let's go out to eat," I offer. "To celebrate your first week on the job. I'm starved."

"This isn't a milestone, Miles. It's an arrangement. There's nothing to celebrate."

"I have homework," Erin says.

"Come on, you two." I lift up my hands. "Live a little."

"You're sure in a good mood. What's going on?" Madeline places her handbag and briefcase on the foyer table.

"Come, let's go sit down." I wave them over to the living room. "Want a glass of wine?"

"I'm going upstairs," Erin says. "If you go out, bring me something back." She turns and heads up to her room, and Madeline strolls gracefully over to me.

"How 'bout an impromptu date night?"

"I'm not really in the mood," she says.

"Come on. It'll be fun. Where's your sense of adventure?"

"What is up with you, Miles? You've been a nervous wreck for the last month or so, and now all of a sudden, you're walking on air."

Am I that transparent?

I hadn't realized Madeline had picked up on my anxiety. The last thing I need is for her to start asking questions.

"Have a seat. I'll get us some wine, and then I'll fill you in."

"You're being quite mysterious, Miles." She shoots me that sly smile, the one from yesterday morning. "I like it."

It brings me back to the long, lingering kiss in the car at school, and I start to feel a different kind of hunger.

"You like it, do you?" I take her in my arms.

"Yes, I do. Keep talking like that and we might not make it to dinner."

Her long auburn waves fall gently forward as she leans into me. I brush the hair back from her face and pull her in for a kiss, and it's even better than the one in the car.

———

I'm lying in our king-size four-poster bed at the close of one of my best days in recent memory, our lovemaking fresh in my mind. Madeline seemed mildly pleased with the news about the donation, although she could not have grasped the importance of it for our future. She was significantly more excited about the news that Brooke was going to be moving on in a few short months.

She knew about the head of school search and the rift that developed among the board members about the decision, and she'd challenged me more than a few times about backing

Brooke for the job. But I couldn't tell her the reason I needed Brooke in the position. It pains me to think that she might have, even for a second, believed the rumors about the affair, and once the statute of limitations has passed, I'll tell her the truth. Until then, I have to have faith that our marriage is strong enough to keep us together. *It certainly felt that way tonight.*

Madeline comes back from the bathroom and slips into her side of the bed. I wrap myself around her, both of us still naked, her long limbs entwining with mine. I drink in the scent of her, wondering what the future will bring. Erin is a senior this year, and very soon she'll be off to college. We'll be empty nesters, and that makes my heart sink a bit. The years seem to be flying by.

"Can you believe Erin's going away to college soon? We only have one more year," I say. "Where did the time go?"

"I know. That's part of the reason I took the job. So I can spend as much time with her as possible before she leaves."

That thought hadn't even occurred to me. She's a great mother, and I marvel at how she transcended her rough childhood, saddled with a needy, alcoholic mother and a deadbeat dad. She practically raised herself, working to put food on the table and help support the family, and I feel a little guilty now for wishing she'd get back into a career. She always said she wanted to be a stay-at-home mom. Now, with the new development project moving forward and the crisis at Falcon Ridge averted, we can afford it.

I pull her into me, hold her tight, and kiss the top of her head.

"Speaking of college, I increased our life insurance last week, like you suggested. You still have to sign the paperwork for your policy," I say.

"Shh, Miles. It's late," she replies. Then she draws my hand to her lips and kisses it, and I fall into a deep, dreamless sleep.

TWENTY-TWO

Cassie

The first week of school flew by, and I have no idea how Dan and whoever he's working with are going to wrap up whatever they're planning by the end of next week. Dan hasn't been very forthcoming about what's going on, although I've been subtly pumping him for information when I can. But then again, we haven't spent much time together, so there hasn't been much opportunity to pry. It's Saturday afternoon, and I'm due to head over to his apartment in about an hour. Maybe I'll get something out of him today.

I've been super busy this week. We've had a ton of meetings. At one of them, I suggested we create a buddy system between the day students and the boarders to make them feel more at home, which was Kimi's idea; they had a similar program at her old school. Brooke loved the idea. I gave Kimi the credit. They gave me all the additional work.

Me and my big mouth.

So now I'm coordinating a pilot buddy program in addition to teaching classes, managing the department, and trying to keep Dan's head above water. Consequently, I haven't had much time for sleuthing or romantic fantasies.

Madeline Kensington came to one of the meetings and introduced herself to all the department chairs. She seemed nice enough, but I could swear I felt an undercurrent of tension when she spoke directly to me, although the words themselves were totally unalarming. The time we met to discuss Erin's grade she seemed fine, and I don't know what could have changed since then. Maybe it's because she's in charge now. Or maybe she's nervous and in over her head. Perhaps I'm misreading her.

But then I remember that I thought she looked familiar when Ed pointed her out to me in the cafeteria that day when I was telling him about Erin's essay. Do we know each other from somewhere? Or did I cut her off in traffic one day...or flip her off, maybe? I'm a California driver, and I really need to be more patient in a small town like this. I've adjusted over the last few months, but I still have my moments. It's possible, I suppose. I can't think of another reason that she wouldn't like me.

One thing is for sure: if there's any animosity between Madeline and Brooke Baxter, they're both doing a great job of hiding it. Madeline seemed totally at ease in front of Brooke at the meeting—gracious, even. Brooke was her bristly self, but no more so than she is with everyone.

Perhaps Ed's right and the rumors about Brooke sleeping with Madeline's husband are unfounded. It's an easy allegation to make against an assertive, successful woman. Sleeping with the boss. Maybe Miles Kensington actually thought Brooke was more qualified than Doug Walker, or perhaps he wanted the continuity of an insider. She's certainly efficient. And smart. And he wasn't the only one backing her on the board.

But she is ambitious. And she can be ruthless. So I don't let myself forget that whenever I walk into a meeting, I might be looking into the eyes of a murderer. Speaking of keeping my guard up, I need to get ready for my session with Dan, so I head into the shower to make myself presentable.

———

I enter Dan's room wearing a tight royal blue t-shirt with a V-neck that shows off my perfect C-cup breasts. They're my best feature, so I decided to lead with them. I'm pretty limited as to what I can wear to a study session followed by an ultimate fighting match. Dressing up is not an option, so I'm going for casual-hot. I've paired the t-shirt with fitted black yoga pants, and I smoothed on some vanilla body lotion that's not too strong. Perfume would be too much of a giveaway. And regardless of what Ed says, I'm not sure Dan feels anything at all for me, so I'll play it cool.

"Hey, boss," he says, holding the door open as I enter the room.

"I'm not your boss," I say when he closes the door behind me. "Not really." I place my computer and files on his desk.

"Yeah, but that's our little secret."

"We're alone."

He flashes me a wry smile. "Romano. Didn't they train you to never break cover until you're sure it's secure?"

He seats himself in one of the two chairs facing his desk. It's a small desk, so we'll be very close together, and the fact that our arms will soon be touching sends a shiver up my spine.

"Huh?"

"We sweep for bugs in my apartment, but you never know about the hallways."

"I don't remember what they told us. But then I was only thirteen at the time. From what I recall, they pretty much left us alone, after we settled into our new life."

"Wow." His eyes widen. "That had to be so hard for you, Cassie. I don't know if I could have done it."

I pull out the other chair and sit down next to him. "What do you mean? You're doing it now."

"But this is by choice. And I'm an adult. When I think back on myself in middle school. What it would have been like to leave everything and start over. I can't even imagine."

"I think I was pretty much in shock for much of the first year. Starting over wasn't the worst part. Lots of kids move around. It was the fact that I could never contact my friends again. And we could only see our relatives through supervised arrangements. I really missed talking to my grandparents on a regular basis."

"I'll bet." He nods. "My grandmother's hanging on by a thread, which is why I came back to the States."

"Are you still trying not to break cover, or is that part really true?"

"That part is true, unfortunately." He sighs. "The less you have to make up, the better."

"Yes, that's why I got to keep my first name."

"So, you've always been Cassie."

"Yeah," I say. "Their one concession." I recount for him the conversation with my parents and our handler, who ended up taking my side. "How about you?"

"Dan Moralis is my real name. We don't always need an alias. Like I said, the less you have to fabricate, the better. It's easier to hide the fact that I'm FBI than it is to fake an entire persona on social media."

I nod, but I also recall that his social media presence was pretty thin for someone in our age range.

Then he tells me that he actually worked as an English teacher before joining the bureau. He did a stint with Teach for America in El Paso—he's apparently bilingual—and got recruited into the FBI somehow when he was there. How that went down is a bit unclear. And now I feel like a snob for having an attitude about his AP teaching skills. The guy was in the trenches, trying to make a difference. *What difference am I making?*

"Moralis. Is that…Spanish?"

"Greek," he says.

We're quiet for a bit. Then he takes a deep breath. "This is nice."

"What's nice?"

"Having someone I can really talk to about…myself. Know what I mean?"

"I do," I reply.

I haven't experienced this with anyone outside my family since we fled, simply being free to be myself, and not having to worry about saying something wrong. And I wonder if he's feeling anything besides friendship for me as my heart flip-flops around in my chest.

Then he reaches for his computer and opens it. "Speaking of not blowing my cover, we don't have much time, so we should probably get started."

"Right. Of course."

We get to work, and I can see it will take a bit longer than last time because, in addition to the lessons, I also have to double-check his grading of the first assignment. After about an hour and a half, we've gotten through his lessons for next week, but we haven't even started on the grading.

"Does this all seem doable?"

"Yes. It'll get me through the week. One week at a time is about all I can handle, but it's getting easier."

"Okay, we can start on the grading now."

He rolls his eyes. I'm not thrilled about more back-crunching work, either, but we need to get through it.

"Unless you want to break this up with something more… physical?"

I have butterflies in my stomach, and I wonder about his choice of words. *Did he mean anything by it?*

"Great idea."

We stand up, and I'm a little nervous.

"It's Saturday. You want a beer to loosen you up a bit?"

"Sure," I reply. "A beer sounds great."

He heads to the fridge and takes out two bottles of Heineken while I stretch my back out a bit, then he pops off the caps and hands me a beer.

"Cheers," he says.

"Cheers." I take a cautious sip, and he more or less chugs a third of the bottle.

"Okay." He plunks down the bottle. "Let's go over the two moves from last week."

We run through them both, and he seems impressed. "You're a quick learner," he says.

I reach for my beer and take a few more sips. It's working to build my confidence. "I do my homework. I practiced a bit on my own last week."

"Were you always such a star student?"

"That's me. Teacher's pet." I shrug. "How about you?"

"I was a bit of a…rebel." He offers me a cheeky grin.

"You don't say."

"Hey!" His brow furrows. "I didn't think it showed."

"Oh, it shows."

"Okay, hotshot. We'll learn one new move today, the choke hold. It can be a bit disturbing, but I want to go over it because it's easy to get out of if you know what to do. But if you don't, it can be deadly."

Deadly.

That sobers me right up.

We watch the training video, and I see what I need to do. When his hands are around my neck, I should hike up my elbows, twist to one side, and sandwich his arms between mine. Then I'm supposed to jam my elbow back into his face.

"Okay, let's try it."

We practice slowly, so I can learn the moves. Then it's time to try it for real. Dan instructs me to look away, so I can't see when he's coming for me. I wait for what seems like a long time, but it's probably only a minute or so. And then he lunges at me and grabs me by the throat, a lot tighter than the last time. My claustrophobia kicks in, and I feel my adrenaline surge. Then my survival instincts take over. I hike up my elbows, crush his arms between mine, and jam my elbow back into his jaw before I can even process what's happening.

"Agghhh," he cries out. "Holy shit, Cassie!" He steps back and rubs his jaw while I stand there, totally in shock.

"I'm...oh my god. I'm so sorry. It was pure reflex."

"Sorry? Don't be sorry. That was perfect. Now get me some ice. I need to minimize the visuals. My cover doesn't include ass-kicking."

"Right."

Soon we're sitting on his loveseat, finishing our beers while he holds a bag of ice to his jaw. I haven't eaten in a while, so the alcohol is going straight to my head. I may have actually impressed him with my face-injuring move.

Feisty Cassie.

We still have to go over his grading, but I'm not going to be the one to point that out. Instead, we continue our conversation, and I learn a bit more about him, at least the parts he can share. Unlike me, he's not an only child. He has a brother and a sister, parents, and a large, extended family somewhere, but he's not saying where. Some light jazz plays in the background, which he must have turned on while I was getting the ice.

When he puts the bag of ice down, I see the faint outline of a bruise forming on his jaw.

"You've got a little parting gift there." I point towards the mark.

"Where?"

I reach for his face with my hand and lightly stroke the spot. "Right...there."

When he covers my hand with his, his big, brown puppy dog eyes meet mine, and I see a longing I didn't notice before. We lean into each other and our mouths meet. There's a slight hesitation, and then he runs his fingers through my hair and pulls me into him.

We kiss for what feels like an eternity, exploring each other, slowly at first and then with increasing intensity. He caresses me with his strong hands, and I love the feel of them on me. I run my hands over his firm, muscular body as I take in his scent, the one that's been driving me mad. All my nerve endings are tingling. But it feels natural, not awkward, and I want him like I've never wanted a man before.

Then his phone buzzes. He stops in his tracks and pulls away from me. I wonder if I've done something wrong. We both take a breath, and he brushes himself off. Then, to my shock, he picks his phone up and starts scrolling through his messages. After a bit, he looks up at me.

"We should probably call it a day, don't you think?"

Call it a day? Are you insane?

I don't want to appear overeager, so I have no choice but to agree with him, but I have no idea how to interpret what just happened.

"Um, sure. It's getting late."

Like we have anywhere to be.

I don't bring up the fact that we haven't gone over his grading yet. I just gather up my things and start to head out, more confused than ever.

"Okay, so...I'll see you around," he says and gives me a half-hearted shrug.

What the hell?

I don't give anything away about how I'm feeling. I just walk to the door and grab the knob.

"Don't forget to cover that bruise up with something. You don't want to break cover," I say.

And then I open his door and walk out of the room.

TWENTY-THREE

Madeline

It's Monday, the second week of school, and the start of my second week on the job. I'm getting a little restless, but I need to be patient. I'm hoping today will be the day they come for her, as I am every day. I don't know for sure when it will be.

Soon though.

I've dropped enough breadcrumbs. And that puts a smile on my face because thinking about what Brooke has coming to her is the only way I can keep my sanity. That, and the knowledge that I have what she wants and that she'll never get it. The only way I can smile politely at her caustic remarks is by picturing her being hauled off in handcuffs and then trying to survive in state prison. She thinks she's so tough, the way she bosses everyone around at this place, but she has no idea what tough is. I'd survive better in prison than she would, with her cushy upbringing and Ivy League pedigree. I'd crush her in a second if I had the chance. I bet she won't last a day in prison.

I hear someone breathing and look over towards my office door, and I feel my mood lighten. "What can I do for you, sweetie?" I wasn't lying to Miles about my reasons for taking this job, and I'm delighted to see my daughter in the doorway.

Yes, my number one reason for getting myself installed as head of school at Falcon Ridge was to take down Brooke Baxter, the woman who's trying to ruin my family, and fix my husband's mess. But a major side benefit is getting to spend time with Erin. I'd do anything for her. In fact, she's the reason I got myself into this situation in the first place. I need to protect her, so that's what I'm doing. Unlike my own mother, I won't let that whore steal my daughter's father, and I won't let us sink into poverty.

"I heard about that buddy program with the boarding students. I think I want to do it. Is that okay?" Her brow furrows as she awaits my response.

I'm somewhat pleased by the fact that she likes to seek my approval on these matters, although I realize she needs to learn to stand on her own two feet. We've got another year or so before she goes to college, so I'll work on moving her in that direction.

"Of course it's okay."

"I might have to back down on some of my extracurriculars to make time. How will it look for college, if I drop out of yearbook now? And do you think they can find someone to replace me?"

"Don't worry about yearbook, Erin. They'll find someone."

"I feel bad, dumping my work on everyone."

My daughter, the compassionate one.

She certainly didn't get that from me. I know people tend to like that in a person, but I'm worried the world will eat her alive. She needs to think of herself more and not always worry about what people think.

"Forget yearbook. The buddy program will look better to colleges. It's more like volunteer work, and you're a little thin on that."

"Okay. I'll tell Ms. Romano I'm in. I need to get to class."

"Love you."

"Love you too, Mom."

Ms. Romano.

Ms. Cassie Romano. The busybody who emailed me and had me meet with her about Erin's essay exam. The one who insinuated that my daughter might be upset about something.

And the one person who might be able to screw things up for me.

I've been keeping a close eye on the Romano girl. I know she was friends with Kimi Choy, so she's been on my radar for a while, even before she saw me at school, the morning Choy had her unfortunate accident. I don't know who Choy called from the train station, and I've been going over and over it in my head to try and figure it out. There's a chance it could have been Cassie Romano, but I don't think so. I heard her clearly on the phone. *I have some information for you*, she said. *Call me as soon as you get this.*

It sounded like someone had put her up to something, and I don't think it was Romano; it's not something you'd say to a friend. But after I heard the call, I knew I was doing the right thing. She knew something about what Miles and Brooke were plotting, and she was planning to tell someone, someone who could hurt our family. And that was just the tip of the iceberg. If they found the videos, they'd keep looking. And then they'd find out everything, and I wasn't ready for that...not yet.

I could have taken her phone, I suppose, but that would have aroused suspicion, and I needed more time before the police started to investigate. I was hoping they'd rule it an accident, and they did. I stayed at the top of the stairs long enough to see her head crack open, so I knew she wasn't going to live to say that she'd been pushed. But I had to get out of there quickly and return Brooke's car, and a missing phone would surely indicate foul play.

No, I wasn't stupid enough to use my own car. I know the cameras weren't working at the Cortlandt station, so nobody can place me there. Still, I had to leave before I was seen by another passenger, and I needed to get Brooke's car back to school. I also needed more time to plant the evidence—the evidence that will convict Brooke Baxter of not one, but two crimes. As I said, it was a bit of an impulse move that day, and not my best work in terms of planning. I had bad PMS that week and my nerves were shot. I wanted them to think it was an accident at first to buy me some time while I executed my plan to get rid of Doug Walker and planted the rest of the evidence on Brooke. And then when I had all the pieces in place, I called in an anonymous tip to get the police to start looking into it.

I know Brooke has no alibi for that morning. I know this because she was with my husband at the motel where they meet, when he's supposedly out "jogging," well before dawn. That's how I caught him. I guess evenings are too hard to pull off with a wife and kid at home.

When I heard Miles leave that morning, I pretended to be asleep. I knew they were meeting from the hours of recordings I have at my disposal. I have to sift through a lot of dull material before I find something useful. It takes time and it's tedious, but I have a lot of time on my hands. I knew Miles would be gone for a few hours, so after he left I headed over to the school.

My plan was to watch for Kimi Choy and follow her, to make sure she didn't go to the police or do anything stupid while she was leaving town. I knew she was planning to depart early that morning from the letter she'd left in Brooke's box—the one that caused Brooke to blow a gasket and start panicking. I wasn't planning to kill her, at least not at first. But when I arrived on campus, an idea popped into my head. *Maybe I can get rid of her and frame Brooke.*

I know Brooke takes an Uber to and from the motel so people don't see her car there and get suspicious, and I was reminded of that when I saw her car at school sitting in its usual space. I also know that she usually stays until late checkout at the motel, to get some distance from work, long after Miles has left, so she'd have no alibi. Miles is always home around seven from his "jog."

I can't stay past seven. My wife will get suspicious. I actually heard him say that on one of the recordings like he was pulling a fast one on me. He's no James Bond, that husband of mine.

I have a key to Brooke's residence because we lived there for a few months when our house was getting renovated years ago. I started keeping it on me when I found out about them sleeping together. I've always known I was going to do something to her, I just didn't know what it was going to be. I held on to her key, waiting for the right opportunity to present itself, and that morning, it finally happened.

So, I entered her apartment, found her spare car key, got in her car, and waited for Kimi to come out. At first, it felt like a game. I'd never done anything that crazy before. I'd stolen stuff in my youth, mostly out of necessity. I'd sent thugs to beat up my enemies, like my ass-pinching boss. With looks like mine, I've never had to get my hands dirty. But the thought of what I was about to do sent my adrenaline surging. I felt truly alive in a way I'd never experienced before. It was intoxicating.

But I wasn't sure if I could actually do it—kill her, I mean. Or if an opportunity would even surface. Nevertheless, I had to try. Especially with the possibility of pinning it all on Brooke. It was just too tempting. It was risky though. If I had it to do over again, I probably would have done things differently.

It all worked out, except that by the time I got back to campus with Brooke's car, I had to pee really bad, so I ran into the admin building, and that's when I saw Cassie Romano—and she saw me—but not anywhere near Brooke's car. I'm not even sure she knows it was me. I had my hair in a ponytail with a baseball cap on my head, and I was wearing sunglasses. And we hadn't officially met yet. But I've been keeping an eye on her, just in case.

Meanwhile, someday soon, they'll come with a warrant. They'll search her office, her computer, and her apartment, they'll check the GPS from her car, and they'll haul Brooke Baxter off to the police station.

And I'm living for that moment.

TWENTY-FOUR

Cassie

Nearly a week has passed since my mind-blowing make-out session with Dan, and I'm still trying to figure out what happened and what, if anything, our kiss meant. I got a text from him the following day, saying he had to go off campus, so he opted to email me some of his graded papers and had me give him feedback that way rather than in person. But then, he did confirm we'd meet again the following Saturday, which is tomorrow, so I really don't know what to think.

We haven't run into each other much this week, although the few times we did, he's been friendly. But we were always in front of other people. I'm thinking he's probably regretting the kiss. I probably should be regretting it too. I mean, where could this even go? I'm sure he'll be leaving when they wrap up the case, and that's supposed to happen soon. I know I said I was fine with a casual fling, but I'm not sure if I can keep my emotional distance from him. It's probably wise to cut it off before it gets even more intense. Maybe he feels the same way.

But then, I also got to thinking, what if he's not single? He could have a wife and kids somewhere, for all I know. Maybe that's who the text was from.

Anyway, I need to head to class. I walk out my door and into the hallway and run smack into him. It's our first time alone together since last Saturday.

"Hey!" Dan says this with a nervous smile like he's not thrilled to run into me. He seems to feel awkward in front of me now.

I'd be lying if I said I wasn't disappointed, but then what did I expect? That he'd run up to me, take me in his arms, and start making out with me right here in the hallway?

"Hey back."

"Heading over?"

"Um...yes."

Could this conversation get any more stilted?

"I'll walk over with you," he offers.

"Sure."

I'm not reading much into this. Anything else would be even weirder and more awkward. We continue in silence out the front door and towards the main part of campus. I look over at him, trying to read his expression. His jaw is tight and his lips are pressed together. *Is he angry? Is he upset about something?* If so, I don't think it's directed at me.

"You feel okay about the rest of the grades?" I ask, trying to make conversation.

But he's not paying attention to me. His eyes are focused forward, and there's an intense look on his face. And a moment later I understand why, when I see two police cars drive up to the main entrance. The officers aren't using their sirens, but they don't park in the guest spots. Rather, they stop directly in front of the building, turn off their engines, and wait in their cars.

I look over at Dan. He raises his eyebrows and gives his head a slight, nearly imperceptible nod. I understand instantly: it's happening, and I need to be careful not to give anything away.

We continue walking slowly towards the gathering crowd, and we're soon within earshot of other people. I think about what someone would say if they weren't already clued into this.

"What's going on?" I ask, turning to him.

He shrugs. "No idea."

———

It's midday, and there hasn't been much news beyond the fact that the police arrived with a search warrant and are executing it. Apparently, that takes time. The officers are mostly staying in the administration offices, so we're not really privy to what's happening. I haven't seen Dan since this morning, and I panic, thinking about how I'd feel if he simply disappeared. But that's silly. He'll probably stay on for a while longer, not just vanish with the police cars later today. Then I realize I really have no idea how all that will work, no clue how and when they extract an undercover agent from an assignment.

We just disappeared one day. Why would this be any different?

As I enter the cafeteria, Ed's already at a table, so I place my backpack next to him before I head over to grab my lunch.

"Any idea what's going on?" I ask.

"Nothing concrete, but I have my theories."

"Let me get some food, and then I'd love to hear them."

My appetite seems to be on hold today, but I feel like I should eat something. I get my usual salad and roll, but I add some grilled chicken because I need some protein. I know Dan has a free period now. I don't see him anywhere, and I wonder if he's involved with what's happening in the admin building, or if he's still keeping his head down. Dan's case is federal, and they're local police, so I'm thinking it's probably the latter, although I don't know for sure.

I plop down across from Ed with my tray. "So, what's your theory?"

"Probably something sexual. That's the only thing I can think of that would bring the local police to campus. Some kind of financial crime wouldn't surprise me, like embezzlement, but I think they'd handle that more discreetly."

"Sexual?"

"Improper relationship with a student."

"Oh...gross. I sure hope not. Can people really be that stupid? In today's world?" I play along, but I'm not really acting. The thought of it makes me sick, and I'm glad I know it probably isn't that. But that sort of thing can still happen. And although it's not the same as having a murderer on campus, it creeps me out in equal measure.

"I guess we'll find out. If nobody gets walked off campus today, then it's probably financial."

I'm sort of surprised that after two deaths, Ed's not putting two and two together. I thought it would be more obvious, but I suppose most people just accept what the authorities tell them. I remember how taken aback he was when I brought it up during our field trip, so I don't mention it, both to preserve my cover and our friendship. If I hadn't gotten Kimi's letter, I'd probably be accepting it at face value too, and I'd probably be better off that way.

Meanwhile, I've been looking around for Brooke Baxter. She's the most likely murder suspect as far as I'm concerned, and I haven't seen her all day. But then, I wonder how this sort of thing works. It's not like there's a gun or a knife or some obvious murder weapon they can find in her office, and even if there were, she's not stupid enough to keep it there. Kimi died from a fall down the stairs, and Doug had a heart episode. Perhaps it's just a fishing expedition, and it's got nothing to do with Brooke. Maybe they're after a bigger fish, like someone with dirty money to launder, or they're looking into the financial irregularities they mentioned at the station.

I look up and see Brooke entering the cafeteria alone. She's not in handcuffs, so I'm thinking she's not their target today. Nobody's paying any attention to her as she gets her tray and gets in line. Then I see Dan walk in, and my spirits lift a bit. I watch as he steps into line and gets his lunch. A few minutes later, he comes and sits with us.

"Any news?" he asks.

"Nothing," Ed replies, before expounding on his various theories while Dan plays the part of the clueless new guy. I'm impressed by how good he is at this, and I remind myself that I don't know him very well at all. I can't let my imagination fill in the parts of him I don't know with romantic fantasies of who I want him to be. When we leave for our afternoon classes, I have no answers, just more unanswered questions. And not only about the investigation.

TWENTY-FIVE

Miles

Just a short while ago, I was walking on air, secure in the belief that everything would work out fine. And now, less than a week later, it's all blowing up in my face. *Again.* I was in a meeting in Albany about the new development project this morning when all hell broke loose at Falcon Ridge. I'd had my phone turned off, and when I got back to my car, I heard a slew of dings and chimes alerting me to all the missed messages and voicemails, and I knew something was up.

First, Madeline called, freaking out about the fact that the local police had arrived at school with a warrant to search the administrative offices. Then the incoming board chair called, demanding some answers about what was going on, as if I would know any more than he does at this point. And finally, there was a message from a Detective Robinson, asking me to call him immediately. One person I haven't heard from all day is Brooke.

It's nearing noon, and I've got about another hour's drive ahead of me. I call Butch MacDonald to give him a heads-up about this turn of events but get his voicemail. In my message, I give Butch a brief rundown of what I know and tell him to call back immediately. Then I call Madeline and tell her not to panic and to simply cooperate with the police, but I don't offer to come see her. Rather, I say I'll be home around dinnertime. I need some time to figure out how to handle this before I see her. Then I scan the news channels to see if I can pick up any breaking stories about this. There's nothing, which for some reason makes me even more nervous. My palms are sweaty, and I grip the steering wheel tightly as the scenarios run through my mind, most of them horrific, but one that's not so bad.

Maybe it has nothing to do with me.

I'm the board chair, so any legal issue at the school would land in my lap. And I try not to panic about the fact that the police want to talk to me. Nothing good can come from that. I need to call the detective but wonder if I should get a lawyer first. That could make me look like I have something to worry about, but then everyone says you never talk to the police without a lawyer present. Then it dawns on me that as a representative of the school, it would be prudent to get the advice of the school's legal counsel, so I punch in her number.

———

Tammy Jenkins, the lead attorney for the school, meets me at the police station a few minutes early, and we plan a quick strategy before heading inside. We've met many times, and I know she's competent in civil liability, which is what a school like Falcon Ridge is mostly concerned about, but I'm not sure she's the right person for a criminal investigation. *She's better than nothing though.*

"So, what do we know?" I ask.

"We know little to nothing," she replies, and that doesn't make me feel very secure.

"What did they take?"

"As far as we know, mostly computers and files."

I feel my heart race a bit. That sounds financial to me.

"Are they questioning anyone else?"

"Brooke Baxter. They already have, and she chose to retain her own counsel, so I have no idea what they talked about."

Crap. It's happening. What if she's already flipped on me?

But all of this police muscle seems a bit like overkill for an investigation into invoice padding. I must be missing something. Then I think back to my suspicions that Brooke might have done something to Kimi Choy.

A murder investigation would certainly merit this kind of intensity.

We get seated in a room that, thankfully, doesn't look like the ones I've seen on crime shows, and I'm hoping that's a good sign. No one-way mirror, no bright lights. It looks more like a typical, if dreary, conference room.

"I'm Detective Robinson. Thank you for coming in so quickly." He's sitting across the table from me, leaning back in his chair.

"Of course. Can you tell me what this is about?"

"We need to ask you some questions."

I look at the lawyer, and she nods.

"Go ahead," I say.

He leans in now. "Where were you on the morning of December tenth between the hours of six a.m. and nine a.m.?"

"Where was I?" This is a very specific question, and I feel my throat tighten as I grasp the implication.

"Yes. Where were you? It's a simple question, Mr. Kensington."

"Why?" I'm stalling as my mind races to figure how to play this.

"We ask the questions here. Do you need me to repeat it?" The detective's jaw tightens, and then he sits back in his chair and crosses his arms.

"December tenth? It's hard to remember, offhand. I, ah, I don't have my planner with me."

"Maybe I can refresh your memory a bit. Brooke Baxter claims she was at a motel with you that morning. The morning Kimi Choy was found dead."

I feel my stomach sink. It's worse than I thought. I look over at the attorney, who's probably never handled a criminal case in her life, and instantly regret not retaining more appropriate counsel. She looks even more shocked than me, and totally out of her element.

"May I have a moment alone with my client?" she asks.

"Certainly."

When the detective leaves, I inform Tammy that I was at a motel with Brooke from about five-thirty to six-thirty that morning and that I was home by seven. Her eyes widen a bit, but thankfully she doesn't dwell on that revelation.

"Can you prove that?"

"Yes. My daughter was home with me. We ate breakfast together. My wife has her yoga class then, and it's our routine. They can check the GPS on my car. I have nothing to hide."

She advises me to tell the detective everything I just told her, and she calls the detective back in. The detective has a pretty good poker face, except for when I disclose that I was home from the motel by seven, having breakfast with my daughter. That makes the detective's brows rise up a bit, and I take that as a sign that this conflicts with what Brooke said. I figure Brooke's probably trying to use me as an alibi, and I realize that if I don't back her story, she'll probably tell them about my financial misdeeds. But that's nothing compared to a murder charge, so I don't think twice about throwing her under the bus. Plus, I was with Erin, so I can't lie.

Then Detective Robinson asks me a strange question. "Do you recall seeing Brooke Baxter's car at the motel that morning?"

"Her car?" I put my hand to my forehead, trying to think back. I shake my head. "No. I didn't see it. But I can't say for sure that it wasn't there."

Then the detective thanks me and tells me I'm free to leave.

I breathe a sigh of relief, and try to think positive. As I'm walking to my car with Tammy, she advises me to tell nobody about this meeting, not even my wife, especially since she's the acting head of school. It's Tammy's job to protect the school, and she tells me she will brief Madeline and the board on anything she deems pertinent. For now, Madeline needs plausible deniability, so we agree to keep this interview confidential. And since this matter doesn't seem to concern the school, she informs me she can no longer represent me. As I'm entering my car, she leans in and gives me one last piece of advice.

"If I were you, I'd retain counsel. Soon. Someone with a strong track record in criminal defense. This won't be the last you hear from them. They're just getting started."

———

I didn't know what to do with myself for the rest of the day, so I drove to the other side of the river and had a meal in a cute little town called Cold Spring. It dawned on me more than once that afternoon that I might be losing it because that didn't seem like a normal reaction to what was happening, but it's what I felt like doing, and if there was any possibility I was going to prison soon, I was going to make the most of the time I had left.

I'd been avoiding Madeline all day. Since I'd already lied to her and said I wouldn't be available until dinnertime, I couldn't go home yet anyway. I was still waiting for a call back from Butch MacDonald, and the radio silence was making me even more nervous. After lunch, I strolled around the town for a bit, savoring the ability to simply be spontaneous and free, to walk around and do whatever I wanted, something people in prison surely miss.

Now I'm sitting at a bar, keeping an eye on the television set in the corner for signs of breaking news. I pull out my phone and leave yet another message on Butch's voicemail. I see Madeline is calling, but I let her call go to voicemail. I stay seated and finish my beer, then I realize it's time to face the music. I press Play, and my wife's frantic tone brings me back to reality, the reality that life as I knew it is officially over.

"Why the hell aren't you picking up? Things are crazy around here. They just arrested Brooke. For murder." There's a short pause. "Call me!"

TWENTY-SIX

Cassie

As I head over to Dan's room, I try hard to lower my expectations. I'm dying to find out what's happening with Brooke, but I doubt he'll give up very much about that. I'm not as eager to see if he has an explanation for his freakout last weekend, because it seems pretty clear he views our kiss as a mistake.

I try to tell myself it's for the best that things stopped in their tracks with us. That they're probably wrapping up his operation soon, and they'll be sending him to some distant land and I'll never see him again. So the fact that he cut it off will likely save me much greater heartache in the long run. I tell myself that I'm better off this way, but it's not working. I still feel a longing, an ache deep inside that's unfulfilled, and I know it would be worth the emotional risk to fill it, even if it's just for one day.

Still, I didn't go to as much trouble getting ready today. I threw on a plain gray t-shirt that matches my mood, and the same black yoga pants from last week. I knock on his door, and he opens it. I'm having a hard time reading the look on his face as he invites me in. He's smiling, but it's not the kind of smile that reaches the eyes. They look heavy, with dark circles under them that weren't there the last time I was in this room. I can see the bruise on his jaw, and it brings me back to our intimate encounter. He did a good job of covering it up last week at school.

He's good at masking.

"Good work, Romano."

I tilt my head. "Regarding…?"

"You did a great job playing dumb this week."

"I could say the same about you."

"Yeah, well it's my job."

"But I've had more practice," I say. "I've been pretending to be someone else since I was thirteen years old."

Dan looks off in the distance as if he's calculating the years in his head. "I suppose you might be right about that." He shakes his head. "Wow."

"Let's get started," I offer.

If this is how he's going to play it, my casual buddy, I want to get it over with. We sit down and get to work on the lessons for next week. It goes faster this time, and in less than an hour, we've pretty much got everything planned out for next week. He doesn't bring up the self-defense training, but then maybe I don't need it anymore. Maybe the threat's gone, and this will all be wrapping up in the next few days. We're still seated at his desk, and before I lose my nerve and get up to leave, I decide I need some answers.

"So, is it over?" I ask.

"Is what over?"

I hold his gaze for a bit while we rest on my double entendre. Then I answer him. "The operation, Dan."

"No. Not quite. But maybe soon. It depends on what happens with Brooke."

"Do you really think she killed Kimi? And tried to murder Doug?"

"I have no idea, Cass. And if I did, I couldn't tell you anyway. Plus, the murder investigation is up to the local police. I'm interested in flipping her, to see if maybe whoever did it is connected in some way to our larger issue, and much of that part of the operation is above my pay grade. I'm just here to collect information, not to analyze it."

I wonder if he's interviewed her himself, but I don't ask. Probably not. It would be too risky. She could talk and tell someone at school and blow his cover.

"So, has she given up anything of value so far?"

His eyes widen. "I just told you I can't tell you things like that."

I shrug. "Can't blame a girl for trying."

"Okay. I'll say this. Hypothetically speaking, that is. If a person gets bail on a murder charge, it generally means they don't have much evidence against them."

Brooke Baxter made bail and they don't have much evidence against her. Good to know.

Then he explains that as a special agent, he's a cog in the machine and a rather low-level cog at that. His supervisor, the special agent in charge back at his field office, has her eye on the bigger picture, but even she doesn't know everything. This is apparently a complicated operation, the dirty money part, spanning many offices and involving more than a few federal agencies. The murder investigation is not their primary focus.

"And I could ask you the same thing, about Brooke. You've known her longer than I have. What's your take?" Dan asks.

"On…?"

"Is she capable of murder?"

"I mean, anyone's capable of murder, given the right circumstances. I could see a crime of passion, maybe. But I don't see her going after Kimi just because she heard something about Brooke plotting against Doug Walker. Everyone knows she wanted Doug's job. It seems a bit too convenient to me. And she's also not stupid. I don't think she'd take that kind of risk and actually kill Kimi or Doug. Sabotage him? Yes. But kill him? No. I'd say it's more likely one of your shady donor guys you won't tell me anything about."

"Good to know. I'll keep that in mind."

There's a prolonged silence, and it's obvious that Dan is planning to give up as little as possible about the operation. My only options are to leave or change the subject, and I decide on the latter.

"You look a little...off today. Is something wrong?"

He swallows. And then he takes a deep breath.

"Yeah." He pauses. "My grandmother died."

"Dan! I—"

"But you can't tell anyone."

"I'm so sorry. When?"

"Last Saturday."

"Oh my God. Was that the text that you got..." And suddenly it all makes sense.

"Yeah," he says.

I reach for him and he falls into my arms. He hugs me tight against him. We stay like that for a few minutes, and then he releases me.

"I'm sorry I didn't tell you. I shouldn't even be telling you now."

"Everyone at school knows you had a sick grandmother. That's why you came back to the States. You could have taken some time off. Why all the secrecy?"

"They all think she lives around here, but she doesn't. People might ask for the address to send flowers and cards or even attend the services. I can't let anyone know. And I couldn't leave last week anyway. I knew what was going down at school."

"So, you weren't able to attend the services?"

"I'm planning to go home next weekend for them. But nobody can know, okay? I'll just act like it's a normal weekend away from campus. Can you sell that for me?"

"Sure."

"Are you okay with my being gone? I'll have Cory Wilson on standby."

"Who?"

"The marshal."

"Right. Yeah, I'm okay with it. Why wouldn't I be?"

He shrugs.

"I mean, should I be worried?"

"No, I have no reason to think you're in danger. It's just...I said I'd be right next door. And for a few days...I won't be."

"I can take care of myself for two days, Dan."

He brushes his fingers over my cheek, ever so lightly. "I'm sorry things are so complicated."

"It's nobody's fault. You don't need to be sorry."

Then he pulls me in for a kiss. A deep, slow one. He runs his hand through my hair, and then he stops and looks into my eyes.

"What's wrong?"

"I don't want to make promises I can't keep."

"I'm not asking you to make promises," I reply.

"You've been through a lot. I don't want to be just another person in your life who causes you grief. And I'm not in control of my life right now."

"I'm a big girl, Dan. And I know what I need right now."

He rests his forehead on mine and looks into my eyes. "And what's that, exactly?"

"You," I say.

"You're sure?" he asks.

"I'm sure," I reply.

We stand up and he takes me by the hand, then leads me over to his bed. We stand, face to face, and our hands intertwine as we lean in for a kiss. Then he releases my hands, and I feel them reach beneath my shirt and lightly caress my bare back. The tingling sensation drives me mad with desire. He lifts my shirt gently over my head and tosses it on the floor. We undress each other, slowly. And as we climb into bed, I feel a passion for him that's beyond anything I've experienced before.

Soon we melt into one, and I don't want it to end. It's explosive and hot and romantic, all at the same time. When it does end, we stay in each other's arms for a long time, clinging to this perfect moment.

———

Things felt comfortable between us when I left Dan's room after a long, lingering kiss good-bye. He said he needed to touch base with his parents and make travel arrangements for next weekend, so I told him I'd give him some space. He also mentioned that he'd be off campus tomorrow for something mission related, but that's all I know about his work. As far as my sleuthing, I pretty much got nothing this afternoon, aside from the fact that Brooke's out on bail. But at least I have a better handle on where his head's at as far as I'm concerned. I know our relationship is not likely to go anywhere, but at least I'm not confused anymore.

On the way upstairs to the cafeteria for dinner, I run into Ed. I remind myself to act subdued, not like I had the best sex of my life earlier this afternoon. I wonder if he's going to bring up Brooke and what happened this week. He came to her defense when we talked about the rumor that time on the field trip, and I wonder how he's taking this news.

"How's your weekend going?" I figure I'll let him take the lead about where this conversation goes.

"I'm still sort of in shock," he replies.

And he looks it too. His face is paler than usual, and his face looks tense.

"I get that. I think we all are."

"Yeah. And there's something else."

"Something else?"

"Can you keep a secret?"

"Sure." *You have no idea.*

"They want me to step in to fill Brooke's role while she's on administrative leave. They plan to announce it tomorrow, but keep it under wraps until then. I haven't made up my mind yet."

"Well, that's…I mean, it's not exactly bad news, is it? It has to be a little flattering."

"I'm conflicted. It's flattering and it's hard to say no to something like that. But I was planning some big trips this summer. I finally feel ready to get back into life again. See my friends. My family. I don't want to be stuck here all summer. And I don't need the additional stress. It's been a tough year."

I nod. "So, what did you tell them?"

"I told them I'd let them know by tonight."

There's no line in the cafeteria. It's still early, and it's never very crowded on the weekends anyway. But as I pick up one of the brown plastic trays, I realize how completely and totally sick of this place I am.

"Hey, I have an idea. Do you want to get out of here? Go eat in town or something?"

"Absolutely! Great idea," he replies.

It *was* a great idea, and I should do it more often. Ed and I enjoyed a nice Italian meal. Even a mediocre meal at a New York restaurant is better than anything I've had in California. I'm Italian, so I know of what I speak. It's still early when we finish, so we take a stroll around town. I need to walk off some of my penne marinara anyway. We each drank a glass of wine with dinner, so I have to be extra careful not to give anything away. I let him do most of the talking while we hash out the events of the past week.

"I wouldn't be surprised if whatever this is goes back to Butch MacDonald's tenure. He was chummy with Miles and Brooke. And I always pegged him as being a bit shady."

"Yeah, that was before my time."

I make a mental note to run that comment past Dan when I see him. Although Dan probably knows more than Ed about what's going on now, Ed has a longer history with the school.

Does he know that Butch MacDonald was considered shady?

And then we're quiet for a bit. I pull my coat up around my neck as a gust of wind rips through town, and he seems to sense I've had enough.

"Want to get going back to school?"

"Sure," I say.

Then he stops for a minute and turns to me.

"Okay. I'm going to take the job."

"That's great...*boss.*" I smile.

He rolls his eyes. "Hardly."

As we're walking to his car, he's explaining to me what he hopes to accomplish over the next couple of months as dean of faculty, and he's going on about how much he likes my buddy program and how it's working to form bonds between the day and boarding students. I'm only half listening because I'm thinking about Butch MacDonald and the dirty money donations. If the guy's as morally questionable as

Ed thinks, he might just be the kind of person who would do whatever it takes to eliminate a threat, and I wonder if they've questioned him or Miles Kensington.

One thing I know for sure is this doesn't all start and end with Brooke Baxter, and I'm determined to try to help Dan get to the bottom of it, whether he wants me to or not.

TWENTY-SEVEN

Miles

It's been three days since I was questioned, and I haven't heard a word about the case. I retained counsel, but there's been no indication from her as to when or if the authorities will want to talk to me again. I'm sure it will be soon though, and I wish I knew what was happening with Brooke. All I know for sure is that she was arrested and she made bail, which probably means they don't have much evidence. And I have no idea if she's said anything about my financial crimes, or if they're even looking into that.

I'm still thinking about this when I stop into the local coffee shop to grab a latte for the ride to my next meeting. As I enter and get in line, I'm more than a little shocked to see Brooke standing in front of me. I think about walking out but then I change my mind. It might be my only chance to feel her out.

"Hi," I say.

She whips her head around. "You're the last person I want to see. And I shouldn't be talking to you."

"I shouldn't be talking to you, either."

"Wait," she says, her eyes narrowing. "Are you following me?"

"*What?* No."

She reaches the counter, orders, and steps aside to wait for her drink. I'm anxious to keep the conversation going. After I order, I join her, but she moves away from me.

I take a step in her direction. "So how're you doing?"

Her eyes widen, and she leans towards me, keeping her voice down. "How am I *doing*? I have no job. I'm living in a cheap motel because I'm not supposed to leave town. And someone's trying to frame me for murder. *That's* how I'm doing."

"Well, it's not me. Maybe I can help. Why don't you tell me what's going on?"

"You're the last person I want help from. You've done enough."

"I never meant for this to happen."

"Someone called in a tip, Miles. Who else would it be? You certainly *did* mean for this to happen."

"And you think it was *me*? That doesn't even make sense, Brooke. Think about it. I have everything to lose. Why would I want them to look into it?"

She rolls her eyes, but I know she's smart and logical, and I'm certain that what I said made sense to her. And she gave me one valuable piece of information. *Someone called in a tip.* That's how they got wind of this. It wasn't my financial crimes. Maybe I'll be okay if I can keep Brooke in line.

"Did you say anything about...you know?"

"You're unbelievable! Is that all you care about? You make me sick, Miles. And don't worry, I'll do everything in my power to screw you to the wall. I'm innocent, and I'm going to prove it. And then you and whoever did this will go down."

"I had nothing to do with it. I was with my daughter when the teacher was...when she died."

"I guess we'll see about that. And why didn't you tell them that my car wasn't at the motel?"

I'm caught off guard by this question.

"I'm not sure what you mean. They asked me if I saw your car there, and I said no."

"You know I don't usually bring my car. You could have told them that. Why didn't you tell them that?"

"I...what? No, I don't know that. What do you mean? And they didn't ask me that question. My attorney told me not to volunteer any information."

"Right. Save yourself, you narcissistic piece of shit."

"Brooke, I don't want to be enemies. I have a lot to lose too. Please. If you need anything, I'm here for you."

"Go fuck yourself, Miles."

Then she turns from me, grabs her coffee, and walks out the door.

———

Back at home, after my meeting, my head is spinning. I've heard nothing from Butch MacDonald, and it's making me very nervous. I have a sinking feeling that Butch has decided to disappear, and I wouldn't put it past the guy to murder Kimi Choy and try to pin it on Brooke, or even me, for that matter. Butch is the one who educated me about the benefits of offshore accounts and suggested I not ask too many questions about mysterious donors and just accept their generous handouts.

Every school's doing it, Butch claimed.

At this point, I'm not so worried anymore about the financial issues coming to light. They might not even merit prison time. I'm worried about being framed for murder. Maybe I should try to get ahead of it. Tell my attorney what I know. See if I can make a deal. But that could be very risky. If Butch and whoever he's working with already killed two people, I could be next, so I should probably sit tight and wait.

Meanwhile, I wonder if Madeline suspects that something more is going on. She's been oddly quiet. But then she mentioned that Tammy, the school's attorney, cautioned her about talking to anyone about it, let alone me, the board chair. I wonder what she would do if the financial mess came to light. Would she give me a heads-up or let me go down for it and save herself and Erin?

If only I could talk to Brooke some more or find out what she told the police. But clearly, that's not going to happen anytime soon.

I check my burner one more time. Nothing from Butch MacDonald.

Where the hell are you, Butch?

TWENTY-EIGHT

Cassie

There's a storm coming.

A big one.

It's supposed to arrive sometime this afternoon, and last into tomorrow. A nor'easter, not a squall. They supposedly last longer, although there's more warning.

I'm not exactly clear on what I should be doing in preparation. But we got an email saying to make sure to have batteries for our flashlight—*um, I don't have a flashlight*—and to have a three-day supply of dry or canned food and water on hand, along with some extra blankets in case we lose power. Oh, and to take all other "necessary precautions," whatever that means.

We've had storms before, and I felt like they were pretty major ones. But nobody made a big deal about them, so I'm getting really freaked out.

How much worse can this one be?

I take a deep breath and try not to panic. I don't have to drive anywhere. It will only last a day or two. I'm not alone; there's a campus full of boarding students to care for. They won't let anything happen to them. It's Friday morning, and they haven't canceled classes, so I'll have to wait until after school today to drive to town and get provisions.

In the meantime, I need to get going to my first period class. I gather my computer and course materials, stuff them in my backpack, and head out the door. Dan's already left for the weekend to attend his grandmother's funeral, but nobody knows that except me. He kissed me good-bye earlier this morning when I left his room—we decided to spend the night together—and said he'd be back Monday evening. Even so, I'm bracing myself for the possibility that he's gone forever.

I know he can't tell me everything. And like he said, he's not in control of his life right now. Even if he thinks he'll be back Monday evening, anything can happen. Still, the memory of our night together is fresh in my mind, and nobody can take that away from me.

———

Afternoon classes were canceled to give the parents of our day students time to pick them up and get home safely. It's nearing four o'clock now, and Ed agreed to accompany me on a last-minute run to get storm supplies. We enter CVS and gather my things: a flashlight, an ample supply of batteries, some additional gloves and scarves, canned food, and bottled water. Thankfully, most people haven't waited until this late in the game, so there's enough left for me. Then I tell Ed I need to get a few more necessities, and he offers to wait by the register. When I meet back up with him, he's talking to a woman I don't recognize from behind.

She turns around as I approach, and I see that it's Madeline Kensington. Her hair is pulled back into a ponytail and she's wearing a bulky parka. She looks so different with her hair off her face.

"I'm helping our California girl with storm supplies," Ed says. "She's a bit out of her element here."

Madeline offers me a forced smile, and then her face turns serious as she turns to Ed and runs through some of the precautions we need to take for the students, putting most of the responsibility on him. You would think as head of school she'd be staying on campus with us, but from what she said, it sounds like she is planning to ride it out at home.

And as I'm looking at her with her hair pulled back and that intense look on her face, I suddenly realize why she looked familiar when Ed pointed her out that day in the cafeteria.

I'd seen her once before.

It was a weekend morning, and I was headed to the gym when I saw her running into the admin building. I think it was a Saturday, a few weeks before winter break. I remember thinking that she must be a new teacher or dorm worker because I didn't recognize her, and I couldn't imagine who else would be on campus that early in the morning. I never saw her again, and until now, I hadn't really given it much thought.

That explains why, when Ed pointed her out to me at the cafeteria, the day I was telling him about Erin's subpar essay, that although she looked a little familiar to me, I couldn't quite place her. With her long, flowing red locks and a smile on her face, she looked very different than she had that morning sporting a ponytail, baseball cap, and sunglasses. But now that I see what she looks like with her hair off her face, I'm sure it was her that morning. That explains why I had a flash of recognition and couldn't quite place her, but it still doesn't explain the weird vibe I got from her in the meeting the other day, or the fake smile she just gave me.

"I'm so thrilled that Erin joined the buddy program," I say.

Madeline turns to me. "Yes, she's excited about it. You've made quite an impression on her."

Her tone is pleasant enough, but it doesn't match her eyes, which feel as if they're piercing my skull. Maybe she doesn't like that Erin's joined my program? Or she's jealous of our rapport?

"I feel the same way," I reply, as politely as I can. "She's a pleasure to have in class and in the program."

After a bit, she goes on her way. The cashier rings up my items, and I feel much better about the impending storm. Ed and I start walking back to the car, and I begin to shiver. And then I don't feel so confident about it anymore. *If I'm shivering already, what will I do if the heat goes out?* I suppose I can always sleep in a chair in the student lounge. Their building will have heat. We hop in the car, and I'm still freezing.

"Crank the heat, will you?"

"California girls," he says. "Can't take you anywhere."

Ed's gotten through his first week in his new position in one piece, and as we drive back to campus, he confesses he's even been enjoying it a bit.

"It sounds like maybe you don't want this to be temporary," I offer.

He shakes his head. "No. It's temporary. It's definitely temporary. If I were ten years younger, maybe I'd think about it. But that ship has sailed."

I nod, and then I gaze out the passenger window. My mind drifts as I watch the pretty snowflakes float down from the sky. They look so harmless, it's hard to believe they could do much damage.

But looks can be deceiving, and for some reason, my mind goes back to Madeline Kensington and her interactions with Brooke Baxter. Her smiling face. Her friendly demeanor. Was she faking all of it? And why did *I* get that uncomfortable vibe from her, and not Brooke? I'm not the one supposedly sleeping with her husband. It doesn't make any sense, so once again, I try to convince myself that I imagined it. Maybe that's just how she looks when she's tense.

"Ed?" I ask.

"Yes?"

I think about asking him if he noticed anything about the way Madeline was looking at me, but then I stop myself.

"I guess the storm's starting."

The snowflakes are multiplying before my eyes, and they're already covering the ground. They say we could get ten or more inches by tomorrow, and that we very well might lose power. There's a generator to power the student dorms, but the rest of us are pretty much screwed.

And as I'm thinking about what it might be like to be alone on my floor with no lights and no heat, something hits me—although I kind of wish it hadn't—about the first time I saw Madeline Kensington.

I'm pretty sure it was the same morning that Kimi was killed.

TWENTY-NINE

Madeline

I saw the way she looked at me at the store just now. And I'm sure she's put two and two together. Or she will. Sometime soon.

Shit! It's all falling apart.

Meanwhile, I have no idea what Brooke said to the police. You'd think as head of school, I would get more information. But the authorities aren't giving anything up. They told me to "sit tight." I don't even know if they found the evidence I planted in her office. But since she made bail, I tend to doubt it. I put her on administrative leave though. And I told her she needed to move out of her apartment. We can't have an accused murderer working or living on our campus.

I need to calm down.

The worst thing that can happen is that Brooke doesn't get indicted. They'll never trace it back to me, even if I fail to land her in prison. Her career is effectively ruined, so that's something. I have no idea how much they know about the financial crimes. But if they start digging, they'll get distracted with Butch and Miles and all of the other intrigue. It won't even occur to them to look at me. Brooke will probably think it was one of them who framed her. If it even gets that far. I'm so gracious to her. She'll never suspect me. And I was careful about the rest of it, for the most part. I'm sure I'm in the clear.

Except for Cassie Romano.

She can place me at the school that morning. And I'm certain that clicked in her memory when she saw me with my hair pulled back. I saw the flash of recognition in her eyes. And it won't be long before she figures out it was the day of the murder, if she hasn't already. And if she says she saw me there in a baseball cap and sunglasses, they might be able to match that description to whatever camera feed they've picked up along the route to the train station. I know Brooke's car isn't in view of the two cameras at the school. And I was sure I could pass myself off as Brooke for the drive. But if *I'm* placed at the school in a hat and glasses...*crap!* Why didn't I take them off when I went into the building?

I really don't like where my mind is headed right now. As I said, I'm not a monster. But I have no choice. And I've got the perfect way to get rid of her. Once the storm is in full force, I can make my move. And this time, I won't leave any loose ends. I'll need to go to the hardware store one town over to get more supplies. But I have to be quick. The snow is falling harder now, and I can tell it's going to be relentless very soon.

I need to focus. I need to move fast. I don't have much time.

―――――

"You really think you need to be there?" Miles says as I frantically gather my necessities and pack an overnight bag.

"Yes, I do. I'm the acting head of school."

"I'll come with you."

"No, you stay here with Erin. She shouldn't be alone."

"Where are you going to stay?"

"In Brooke's apartment. Or Doug's."

"You have her key?"

"I have all the keys, Miles. Or I can get them. I'm head of school. And it's not her apartment anymore. Remember? She moved out. After she was accused of *murdering* someone." My eyes nearly pop out of my head, but I quickly make an effort to soften my look.

Why is he asking so many questions? I'm getting sick of this.

I don't need him getting suspicious or upset with me, though. I take a deep breath and try to relax my shoulders. Then I walk over to him and rest my hands on his biceps. I rub them gently. And I smile.

"I know you're worried about me, honey. But it's just a storm. It's not a nuclear war. I'll be fine. But I need to show some leadership. We have minors there to protect."

"You're right. Of course." He nods.

Then I give him a kiss, but not a lingering one, because I'm wasting precious time. If it gets too bad outside, I won't be able to drive up the mountain.

"Okay, I have to go."

I grab my things and head out the door. It's not that cold, so the snow should pile up nicely. The flakes are heavier now, and they're multiplying. Sticky and thick, they already cover the pavement in about three or four inches of white powder. It shouldn't be too long before the roads become impassible.

Perfect.

THIRTY

Cassie

The first thing I do when I get home is plug in my phone, which has only about twenty percent of its battery left. I need a new phone, or at least a new battery, but there's not much I can do about that now. Even when my phone is fully charged it runs down quickly. I wish I had taken care of this sooner.

The thought of being stuck here in the dark without a phone makes my heart start to race. It would even if there wasn't a monster storm raging outside my door; I'm totally addicted to my phone. There are no landlines in our rooms, but we do have them in the offices. If worse comes to worse, I could go over there to make a call. That is unless those go out too. Does that happen? I have no idea. I don't even remember what it's like to have a landline, it's been so long.

The second thing I do is load my flashlight with batteries and make sure that it works. Then I put the spare batteries on my nightstand with my pepper spray. I pop a K-cup in my coffee machine and brew a cup, just in case we don't have power in the morning. Cold coffee I can deal with; no coffee isn't an option.

There's some cheese, yogurt, and milk in the fridge, and that will probably keep pretty well. But I eat some of the cheese anyway. I've got canned beans, veggies, peanut butter, and bread, which should be more than enough. Food's the last thing I'm worried about. It's dark already, although it's only around six, and it looks like at least half a foot of snow has piled up already.

I take out all my winter clothing—my down parka, hat, gloves, boots, and scarves—and extra blankets and place them on my loveseat. When I'm all settled in for the night, I open a beer and hop into bed with my computer, which is plugged into the wall socket.

And then my mind drifts back to the morning I saw Madeline Kensington at school, the day that Kimi was murdered. I let my mind wander, trying to assess her mood. It didn't raise any red flags for me at the time. She wasn't frazzled, but she wasn't exactly calm and friendly either. I'd describe her as...preoccupied. Like she had somewhere else to be. And it annoyed her that she ran into me and had to deal with a social interaction.

And then another thought occurs to me. The day Ed pointed her out in the cafeteria was the same day that Doug had his first heart episode. And, although I didn't actually see her at the Christmas concert, she was there that night too, the night he collapsed. She's around campus all the time, so her being there all three times something strange happened is probably only one or two steps more suspicious than my being around all three times.

But still.

If anyone were looking to pin a murder on Brooke Baxter, it'd be the wife of the person she was accused of sleeping with. But then, Dan said this is all tied into some kind of financial scandal. And some mystery donor with money to launder. A jealous wife doesn't really fit that scenario, and

I don't want to make a false accusation that could back-fire on me.

I startle when the electricity goes off for a moment, and my stomach lurches, but it comes right back on. I hear the beep of my microwave, and then my heater starts up again. I'd feel a lot better if Dan were here. I know that Ed's over in the student dorm, as are the two dorm parents, and there are other faculty members on the floor below me. I don't feel much like being social or having to pretend to be somebody I'm not, though. I'd like to call Dan and tell him my suspicions about Madeline, but I can't afford to waste my battery.

I look out the window and see that the snow is falling even harder. Visibility is getting worse from my apartment. I decide to go downstairs and see just how bad it is. I throw on my parka and boots, grab my key, and head down the stairs. When I open the door, the wind is blowing like crazy, and it almost blows the door shut. The snow is so heavy now, I can barely see the administration building and the student center, so I walk for a few minutes in that direction.

But then the lights go out. I hear a scream, but it doesn't sound like a serial-killer's-got-hold-of-me scream, more like a frightened student suddenly plunged into darkness. I can't believe how totally black it is with no outdoor or indoor lights. And of course, I don't have my flashlight with me.

Damn it.

Although we're too far from civilization to have many streetlights on our road, it's eerie to look down from the mountain and see nothing but darkness where I usually see a town full of lights. Then I hear a thumping sound as the generators kick on, lighting up the student center. The rest of campus is still dark, but my eyes start to adjust a bit.

But between the snowfall and the darkness, I can barely see my building, even though I'm not that far away. I know the way though. And it's not far. So I get myself to the front door and soon I'm safely inside. But it's pitch-black in here, and I have to feel my way along the walls to get to the staircase. I carefully make my way up the steps, feeling for each one. The last thing I need is a twisted ankle. I grope my way to my apartment door, feel for the lock, insert the key, and get myself inside.

Once in my room, I locate the flashlight, which will never leave my side again. Then I retrieve my phone and punch in Dan's number. It goes to voicemail. For all I know, he could be on a plane. I leave him a message about my suspicions—the hell with looking foolish—and tell him to call me as soon as he can. I let him know that we've lost power. I'm about to call Cory, my federal marshal friend, when the phone dies in my hand. That's another thing it's been doing lately. Dying when I should have battery left.

Shit.

At least I got a message off to Dan. And thanks to my training, I've memorized both their numbers. Madeline lives about twenty minutes away in good weather. So even if I'm right, I don't have to worry about her tonight. The roads are probably too dangerous now. I open my computer, figuring I'll stream something to keep my mind occupied.

But then I remember that the internet's out. I reach for my Kindle to see what I have downloaded. A romantic suspense novel sounds good, so I start on that, get back to my beer, and settle in for the night. It's still not freezing cold in here, and the walls are fairly thick. I'm hopeful they will retain heat for a while, enough to get me through the night.

After about an hour, I hear a car drive up. My heart leaps at the thought that it might be Dan or Cory or anyone I can trust. Maybe the roads aren't as bad as I thought. It's cooled off a bit in here, and I have a second layer of blankets on me. But it's still tolerable, and I don't really feel like going out in this weather. I need to know who it is, though. And I can't see anything from my apartment.

I throw on my coat and head back downstairs, this time with my flashlight and pepper spray in hand. Outside, it's blowing like crazy, pushing against me. I lean into the wind as I make my way across campus. The snowflakes don't seem so harmless now as they slice into my eyes in unrelenting succession. I furiously bat them away, trying to clear my vision. When I get close enough, I see Madeline Kensington climbing out of her SUV with an overnight bag and a shovel.

My stomach sinks. She's got her back to me. She doesn't notice me standing here, thankfully. I'm surprised when she heads into the administration building rather than the student center. *What could she be doing in her office on a night like this, with no electricity?*

I wait to see what she'll do, ducking behind a pillar so she can't see me. Icicles form on my parka fur and the snow piles higher and higher. Surprisingly, I'm not that cold. My adrenaline is pumping, and I can feel my heart pounding in my ears. After about ten minutes, I see her come out of the admin building and head over to the student center without her duffel bag and shovel.

And then I get an idea.

I'm not confident enough yet about my theory to tell anyone besides Dan my suspicions about her. There's a good chance I'm wrong, and if I say anything at all, I could blow the whole operation. On the other hand, if I'm right, she might be here to eliminate me, because she's figured out that I can place her on campus the morning Kimi Choy was murdered. Which is possible, given the way she was glaring at me in the store today. Maybe that's why she was looking at me so suspiciously. But that seems insane. She'd have to be crazy to think she could get away with it, and she doesn't seem that crazy to me. Perhaps I'm overreacting.

The way I see it, I have two choices. I can wait in my room like a sitting duck, wondering if she wants to kill me or if I'm simply losing it. Or I can go on the offensive and try to figure out what, if anything, she's planning. So, I'll go back up to my room, pack up what I need, and head over to the administration building to see what's in that bag of hers.

While I'm there, I'll see if there's a landline working so I can call Cory at WITSEC and bring him up to speed on my concerns. If there's nothing troubling in her office, I'll go over to the student center and wait out the storm with Ed. If there's anything in her bag to indicate I'm right, at least I'll have a fighting chance. I could even try to leave, if I can't reach anyone. *She got herself here, so how bad can the roads be?*

THIRTY-ONE

Madeline

Ed and the team were so happy to see me. I think it means a lot to them that I'm willing to give up my creature comforts and camp out with them during the storm. It's what a good leader should do. I'm surprised Miles even questioned me. But then, as I said, he's been a bit of a disappointment, generally speaking, and tonight was no exception.

Pretty soon, I'm going to head over and take care of my little problem. I've made my appearance here, and the students are all tucked in for the night, along with the dorm parents. There's not much for me to do. Ed's decided to stay in the lounge and sleep on the sofa. I can't say I blame him.

It's not very late, not even eight o'clock, but the snow is piled high and the wind is whipping across the plateau with a ferocious howl. This is my chance. I heard on the radio that the storm has shifted a bit and might not last as long as they thought, so I don't want to waste this opportunity.

I tell everyone I'm going to get settled in Doug's old residence and to come get me if they need anything. But first, I'm going to head to my office and grab the gun I left there, along with what I got at the hardware store. Shooting her is not my first choice. And if it comes to that, I'll have to improvise. I know people who can get rid of bodies for me. But it's not ideal to involve other people. You never know what they might do once they have something like that on you.

Once I have my supplies, I'll head over to the faculty residence to "clear off the sidewalks." I'll take my shovel so if someone sees me, I have a good excuse for being out and about. Then I'll text her and tell her to come over to the student center because we need her help. When they find Cassie Romano's body down in the valley somewhere, after her tumble off that cliff, nobody will question it. They'll just assume she got lost in the blizzard, trying to make it over there.

California girls.

"Thanks so much, Madeline, we really appreciate you coming out in this," Ed Roberts says.

He's a lovely man, and I made the right choice, promoting him. I'm sure he'll have my back. And I need someone like that around here.

"Of course," I reply. "There's nowhere I'd rather be tonight."

———

When I head into my office to get what I'll need to take care of my little problem, I can tell immediately that something's different.

There's light.

It's coming from my computer, which is sitting open on my desk. I remember opening it to check how much battery it had. But I don't remember leaving it open. I don't remember closing it either, but I feel like it's something I'd do on autopilot, trying to preserve the battery. If I didn't leave it open, it means someone was in here snooping around. That means I'm probably right about Cassie Romano. Because I can't imagine who else it would be. And she's even more of a danger to me than I thought.

I open my desk drawer and grab the gun.

THIRTY-TWO

Cassie

The wind outside is so loud that I only heard her foot-steps when she was almost in the room with me. I didn't even have time to close her computer before cramming myself in the closet and locking it from the inside. I wanted to see if there was anything of value on it, but I hardly got a glance.

I hope she won't notice, but I bet she did.

Inside her bag, I found zip ties, a small, metal, saucer-type sled with a rope attached to it, and some chloroform spray. I'm sure she's planning to use it all on me, which means she's more of a psycho than I thought. How does she think she's going to get away with it? And the spray isn't even the kind of chloroform that can knock you out. It's some kind of watered-down sleep aid. What is she planning to do? Sing me a lullaby and then send me barreling down the moun-tain in a child's saucer?

She's obviously not thinking straight, which makes her even more dangerous. I didn't even have a chance to check if the phones were working. Stupid move not to check them first and call Cory. But I wanted to see what was in her bag before I called anyone so I'd have some evidence to support my theory.

The air is stale in this tiny, cramped space. It's taking all my willpower not to have a complete panic attack. My palms are sweaty and my pulse is racing. I need to maintain control, so I breathe slowly...*in for five, out for ten*. It's a small space. I barely fit in here with this giant parka, which is making me sweat like crazy. But I tell myself I'm not trapped here. I can unlock it from inside as soon as she leaves. I listen and I don't hear anything except the wind.

Maybe she left already.

Then I hear footsteps headed my way. I try to remember the moves Dan taught me. I have my pepper spray, but it's so dark there's a good chance I'll miss her eyes. I'm not sure it's worth the risk. I'll only have one chance, and she might have the shovel in her hand.

Maybe she won't open the door?

But that's delusional wishful thinking. She'll be coming at me from the front, so my best approach is to try to throw her off balance. I attempt to crouch down, thinking that when she opens the door I can spring up and catch her by surprise, but there's not enough space for that. I don't hear footsteps anymore, so I assume she's standing outside the door. I'll have to play it by ear and hope I'm scrappy enough to let my instincts take over.

I hear her turn the knob. It's locked, so it doesn't open.

"Nice try, Romano," she says.

Of course, she has a key.

She opens the door, exposing me. Her red locks look wild, backlit by the glow of the computer. And I'm staring down the barrel of a gun.

Shit.

We never went over gun scenarios. She wouldn't be stupid enough to use it on me. Would she? Even with the wind whipping around, I feel like someone would probably hear a gunshot. And the wind is starting to die down. Maybe I can give us both an out.

My hands go up. "Please don't shoot, Madeline. I'm not a burglar. I can explain."

"Drop the act, Cassie. We both know why you're here."

"Don't do it, Madeline. It's just a matter of time before backup arrives. I'm not working alone."

"You're bluffing," she says.

"I'm not bluffing. I'm working undercover. I know about the dirty money. It's all going down soon. Brooke Baxter's just the tip of the iceberg."

I've struck a nerve.

She looks off to the side for a moment, distracted. Seizing the opportunity, I duck under her arm. Then I start to yell and jump around like a crazy person. I'm screaming like a wild banshee, darting from side to side, trying to disrupt her OODA loop, something I learned during the only useful professional development session I've attended in my entire teaching career.

Flooding the senses of a gunman confuses them, they taught us, which provides an opportunity to get control of the weapon and take them down, or run. I'm not about to flee and leave this nut job free to roam around with a loaded gun, not with a campus full of students. So I hurl my pepper spray at her face, and she flinches.

It worked.

Her gun is pointed down as she looks off to the side while her mind struggles to process what's happening. I swing my leg around and kick the weapon out of her hand. It goes flying across the room and I hear a shot ring out.

She recovers. Then she whips around and grabs me from behind. I slam back into her, trying to execute the move Dan taught me. But she's much lighter than he is, so we both stumble and fall backwards, bouncing off the loveseat and onto the floor.

I'm on top of her, facing up. I need to roll over and pin her down. I manage to flip over on my side. I'm wrestling her for control, and the thick parka isn't helping. Plus, her arms are longer than mine, and they seem to be everywhere all at once. She jabs me in the eye with her finger. My eye tears up, but I manage to roll over and get on top of her.

I've got her pinned to the ground, but I don't know how long I can keep her like this. She's still fighting me, and she's strong. I grab my flashlight from my pocket and raise it, thinking I can strike her on the head and knock her out. She almost slips out from under my grip.

"Don't move!"

Ed's voice calls out to us from behind. And although I can't turn around and see him, I'm pretty sure that directive means he's got Madeline's gun pointed at us. We're down on the floor, so I know he can't really see us or assess what's happening in this cluttered office. I drop the flashlight and pin her down again. It's a very dangerous situation.

"Ed! Thank God! Help me. She's crazy. She's trying to kill me," Madeline calls out.

"Don't listen to her, Ed." I shoot back. "She killed Kimi and framed Brooke. And she tried to kill Doug. Trust me. It's true. I'm working undercover, I swear. Look in her bag. You'll see. She figured it out, and she came here tonight to kill me."

Just then I hear someone walking down the hall. I'm hopeful that it's Dan or Cory or the police. The footsteps sound heavy like they belong to a man. A flashlight illuminates the room as the person enters. I crane my neck to look.

It's Miles Kensington.

I'm screwed.

THIRTY-THREE

Cassie

Madeline's husband stands in the doorway, his face pained and confused as I struggle to hold down his writhing wife, and I wonder if I'm about to be killed.

"It's over, Madeline," he says. "I know everything. The police are on their way."

I breathe a small sigh of relief. But I'm not letting go of her because I don't completely trust him. They could be in this together.

"Miles! How can you do this to me?" Madeline's shrill tone rips through the room, and she almost pushes me off her. I can tell her adrenaline's pumping. I don't know how much longer I can contain her.

"Ed! I'm not sure about this," I call out. "Maybe it's a trick."

"Get your hands up where I can see them, Miles," Ed says. "Now!"

"It's not a trick, Miss…" he says, looking in my direction.

"Romano. Cassie Romano," I say. "Your wife came here to kill me tonight. Look in her bag."

"You can put the gun down, Ed," Miles says. "Ms. Romano's right. That's why I came. That's our gun. She took it from our safe. I came here to stop her."

I turn back to look at them again, although each time I do, I run the risk of losing my grip. But I need to read Ed's expression. His voice is shaky, and I'm afraid the gun might go off by accident if he gets spooked.

I catch his eye. "Ed! No! There's a lot going on, and now's not the time to explain it all to you. They might be working together. Let me tie them both up. Then you can lock the gun in the closet."

I hear faint sirens in the background. Maybe Miles Kensington did call the police. But I'm still not sure his compliance isn't some kind of trick to get control of the gun, so I'm not taking any chances. I have no idea what they'd do if they got hold of it though. There's a campus full of people. They can't kill all of us. Maybe they'd try to escape?

"Fair enough," Miles says.

"Get the zip ties out of the bag and come over here, Miles. Quickly," I bark at him. "I need help securing her hands."

Miles heads over to Madeline's overnight bag and grabs a few zip ties.

"Ed, keep the gun on them and stay calm," I say. "After we have Madeline secured, I'll take care of his hands, and you can put the gun in the closet. Ed, remember, you don't want to be holding the gun when the police come charging in."

"Got it," Ed says.

Madeline's eerily quiet as her husband bends down to help me restrain her. And then she springs up at me with all her might, cracking her head against my chin. She lets out a terrifying yowl, tosses me to the side, and breaks free.

"Get the gun, Miles!" she screams to her husband.

"What? No. Madeline, I said it's over."

"You...*bastard!*" She's frantic now, swinging her arms around. She clocks him in the jaw. "First you cheat on me and now this? If you're not man enough, I'll do it myself."

Then she turns and lunges towards Ed.

"No!" her husband cries out.

But I can see the fear in Ed's eyes, and I know it's too late for her. A shot rings out, and then another one, and Madeline's thrown back. She stumbles and crashes to the floor.

The sirens are getting louder as Miles bends down to tend to his wife, trying to stem the fountain of bright red blood that's gushing out of her.

"Ed, put the gun in the closet," I say. "Now!"

I'm terrified that Ed will get shot if they come in here and get the wrong idea. He does what I say and walks to the closet.

"It locks from the inside. Lock the gun in there."

"Done," he says.

I finally let myself catch a breath. Then I grab the land-line and call 9-1-1 to get an ambulance while Miles continues to put pressure on his wife's shoulder. I'm no expert, but even I can tell it's not looking too good for Madeline Kensington. She's losing a lot of blood. And I don't know how long it will take for help to come. But the snow has let up a bit, so maybe it'll be okay.

"I wasn't having an affair with Brooke," he says to her. "That was a cover. But I did screw up. I screwed up badly. And I'm sorry."

"Miles," she says in a tone barely above a whisper. Then her head rolls to one side and her eyes close.

"Maybe we should step outside," I say to Ed. "Give them a moment." With the gun tucked away in the closet, I don't feel the need to pull the man off his bleeding wife and tie up his hands.

"Sure."

We walk out of her office to give them some space. I realize that I don't know how much I can actually tell Ed, so I say nothing, and we wait in silence as the sirens get louder. He's in shock anyway, so I'm not sure how much he'd be able to process.

I put my hand on his shoulder. "It'll be okay, Ed. I promise. It'll be okay."

He nods.

"Is your cell working?"

"Um, yeah. I think so."

He checks, and it is.

He hands it over to me, and I start to call Cory. But suddenly, I don't feel very well. The phone slips from my hand, and I see Ed's eyes pop open.

"Cassie!" He reaches for me.

A tingling sensation shoots up the back of my head and the room spins.

Everything goes black.

———————

When I come to, I'm told that the police have arrived, along with the paramedics, who are working on Madeline. I'm propped up on the sofa in the lobby of the administration building, and Ed's sitting next to me, holding a cold compress on my forehead.

"You okay?" Ed asks.

"I think so," I reply. "Do I look okay?"

"The color's come back into your face, but your left eye's really red."

"She poked me."

Ed shakes his head.

Now that the adrenaline has worn off, I start to take inventory. I've got some injuries. My shoulder is killing me, and I wonder if she maybe dislocated it. Probably not, or I'd likely be screaming in pain. It hurts, but it's not intolerable. And my shin throbs from where she kicked me, along with the spot where her head slammed into my chin.

Cory's here with us, and I'm comforted by that. Dan must have gotten a message to him. He tells me that fainting was likely a reaction to what happened, a profound but delayed response to all the stress. He assures me I'm fine, and that I've only been out for a few minutes. I'd been feeling so calm; this took me totally by surprise.

After a bit, another team of paramedics arrive and check my vital signs. My blood pressure is a little low, but otherwise they tell me I'm fine. They check my shoulder and say it's not dislocated, but they offer to take me to the ER to have it x-rayed. Cory suggests I go, but I protest. I'd rather wait until tomorrow and see how I feel. In the meantime, Ed offers me some pain meds, which I gladly take.

Snow is still falling. I can see it out the window. But it's not as heavy now, and the winds have died down, but the night's far from over. Ed tells me that the storm subsided, which might just save Madeline Kensington's life. Someone has to tell the others that the school is a crime scene. But one step at a time.

The paramedics cart Madeline out on a stretcher, but I don't see her husband. He must be with the police. Then my mind flashes to Erin. My heart breaks for her when I realize her world is about to come crashing down around her, just like mine did all those years ago when I found out that my parents had secrets, ones that would change my life forever.

We start in on what's sure to be a long night of questioning. I'm not sure how much to tell the officer standing in front of us, a younger-looking guy who has just come over to us and started a conversation with Cory, who hasn't mentioned Dan at all.

I follow his lead and don't break Dan's cover. I tell the officer about Kimi's letter and use that as the explanation for how I got mixed up in this to begin with, which is pretty much the truth. I explain to him that I was simply asked to keep an eye out for suspicious behavior, after I received the letter and sent it to the police.

Then I reveal the fact that earlier today, I remembered seeing Madeline Kensington the morning Kimi died, so I started to put it all together. And when I saw her on campus tonight, I came in here to use the landline and call for help.

I wonder what, if anything, this means for Dan and his assignment. At least the murder of my friend is solved, and I feel better that Kimi and her family will get some justice. But even if this operation's wrapped up for me, my real secret—my true identity—needs to be protected.

For me, it's never really over.

THIRTY-FOUR

Miles

I started to get suspicious when Brooke mentioned that a tip was called in to the police. Who would want to frame Brooke for murder if she really didn't do it? I could only think of one person. And when Madeline left the house, looking frantic, I started looking around for signs that she might have known.

But she's the mother of my child, and there was a part of me that wanted to cover for her, a part of me that wanted to pretend I didn't find a vial of Digoxin in her dresser drawer this evening, along with what looked like some kind of battery pack stuck to the side of the filing cabinet in my study that turned out to be a bugging device. But when I checked the safe and found our gun missing, I knew something terrible was about to happen.

Although it doesn't excuse her behavior, I have a hard time thinking she would have gone this far if she hadn't thought I was sleeping with Brooke Baxter. She obviously snapped, and that's on me. If she lives, maybe I can get her off on some kind of insanity defense later. Clearly, she needs help.

But I had to do the right thing tonight and prevent another innocent person from dying, so I had Erin run over to our neighbor's house with the excuse that I needed to be up at school making sure things were safe. At that point, I wasn't even sure I could make it up there. But then the storm shifted a bit, and I had to try.

I was hoping I was wrong about Madeline or that I could talk her out of whatever she was plotting if I wasn't. I was planning to tell her the truth, that the affair was a cover, hoping I could talk some sense into her.

But I was too late.

They took my wife away in an ambulance a short while ago. She's lost a lot of blood, they said, but she still has a fighting chance. Now I'm about to be questioned by an officer who, mercifully, waited for my wife to be taken away before starting in on me. It's going to be a short conversation.

"I'll tell you everything," I say to the officer. "I want to cooperate fully with the investigation. As soon as I consult with my attorney."

My mind is on Erin and how this will affect the rest of her life. My main objective now is to protect her. To make some kind of deal to keep myself out of prison so I can provide a measure of stability for her. I call my attorney, and she says she'll meet me at the station. For the time being, I decide not to call Erin or my neighbors. My daughter's probably asleep. I decide it's better to give her one final night of peace before I spring all of this on her.

I'm putting all the pieces together as I wait for them to do whatever it is they're doing and head to the station. It seems clear that Madeline was planning to frame Brooke for Kimi and Doug's murder, but what about me? Could she have been planning to kill me? Is that why she asked me to increase the amounts on our life insurance policies?

And then a thought pops into my head, and it's a pretty dark one. I have them occasionally, and I sometimes worry about myself. It dawns on me that if my wife dies tonight, I'll get a very large sum of money. Because I made sure she signed her life insurance policy too.

It's finally time to face the music, so I head out with the officer, determined to do everything in my power to protect Erin. That's one thing Madeline and I have in common. We'd both do anything to protect our daughter.

THIRTY-FIVE

Cassie

Three weeks have passed since that horrible evening, and we're all still processing what happened. My shoulder's still a little sore but much better. I didn't dislocate it, and the bruises are healing up nicely. Ed's feeling a little better knowing that he didn't kill Madeline Kensington, but he's still pretty shaken up.

I know nothing about the dirty donors or the financial investigation, but then that's not really my concern. As for the murder investigation, Madeline recovered, and she and Miles have decided to cooperate and try to make deals rather than fight the charges. He's been released, but she's being held without bail.

Turns out I was right about Madeline and what had just happened when I saw her the morning Kimi was murdered, sporting a baseball cap and sunglasses. Her actions seem to have stemmed from her outrage about her husband and Brooke Baxter having an affair.

Madeline took Brooke's car, followed Kimi, and pushed her down the stairs because she knew Kimi had gotten wind of their plot to bring down Doug Walker. Then she framed

Brooke for the murder and went after Doug to cover up her husband's financial crimes.

That part is a little fuzzy to me. Doug was taking Digoxin for his heart problem, and she was slipping him extra medication, crushed up and put into his coffee or whatever. I did some research and learned it's considered a risky drug. The right amount can help a heart patient, but the wrong amount can cause more cardiac symptoms or even kill a person.

But he's back now, leading the school, much to everyone's shock and delight, so either she didn't intend to kill him or she screwed up the dose.

Ironically, Brooke and Miles Kensington weren't even having an affair, or so they say. That was a cover for their meetups. They were plotting to get rid of Doug Walker, which I already suspected from Kimi's letter.

Walker was about to uncover some kind of financial misdeeds that Miles Kensington engineered with the old head of school, Butch MacDonald, who seems to have disappeared off the face of the earth. I'm still not sure exactly what they did or how it's connected to dirty money donations. That's the part Dan can't share with me, but at least I got some closure on what happened to Kimi.

Brooke has been cleared of all charges, even the ones connected to the financial transgressions. Miles Kensington swears she had nothing to do with any of the financial crimes. He claims that he coerced her to go along with his plan to get rid of Walker by promising her the job if she went along with it, and threatening to ruin her career if she didn't. He made a statement to that effect, which was shared with the entire school.

She made some kind of deal, told the police everything she knew, and now she's taking time off. I'm not sure I believe him about her innocence in all of this, but it's interesting that he made an effort to clear her name.

I'm not sure what's happening with him. He's stepped down as board chair, obviously, and he's a free man for now. Madeline, on the other hand, I'm sure will do prison time but not as much as she would have if she'd been convicted at trial. They haven't finalized that just yet, and she's been locked up since she got out of the hospital. I'm surprised she's not trying for an insanity defense, which makes me think she might know more about the dirty money donations and has a card to play.

And I hate to say this, but I'd feel a little better if she were dead. She's obviously a psycho. I worry she may be carrying some kind of vendetta against me. I know people can order hits from prison, and she seems like the type who'd rise quickly in the hierarchy.

But then, I'm sure I'm not the first one on her hit list. Maybe Brooke didn't sleep with her husband, but I bet she tried. I saw the way she looked at Miles, and I'm sure Madeline did too. And how can anyone know for certain what happened all those times they were alone together in a motel room? I bet she's also pissed that he threw himself on his sword for Brooke. I figure as long as Brooke Baxter's still breathing, I'm probably okay.

It's not quite lunchtime, but I head up to the cafeteria to chill for a bit. I see Erin Kensington sitting at a table near the window, gazing out at the view. She came back to school earlier this week, but I haven't had a chance to talk to her. I walk up to her table.

"Can I have a seat?"

"Sure," she says.

"Listen, Erin. I know this must be a terrible time for you."

"No. You don't know. Nobody knows."

"Some people do, Erin."

She rolls her eyes.

"I know you're probably confused. And angry. And scared. And you don't know who to trust. But I want you to know, you can always talk to me."

"O-*kay*," she says, like I'm the one millionth person who's said something like that to her in the past three weeks.

This isn't going the way I planned, because I'm afraid to say too much. Then I decide to stop thinking about myself as the grown woman I am now and reflect on my younger self. I think about how it would have felt if I'd had someone to talk to during that difficult time in my life. Someone who knew exactly what I was going through. And I decide to take a risk.

"Can you keep a secret?" I say.

This seems to intrigue her.

"Sure, I guess. It depends. What's it about?"

"It's about me."

She flashes me a wry smile. "Did you kill someone too?"

I can't help but laugh out loud. She's got a dry sense of humor. That's what makes her such a great writer, along with her impeccable sense of timing.

"No." I shake my head. "It's about my parents."

"Oh."

"I can't tell you too much, and please don't share this with anyone. But I can tell you that I was in a similar situation when I was even younger than you. I found out they had secrets. Big ones, that they were hiding from me. And I resented them for it for years."

"And you're telling me this...why?"

"Because I know you're angry. But if you can try to find a way to forgive your parents, it's better for you. Your dad is all you have right now, and I know he loves you. They both do. Make the most of your time with him. Try to get past the anger if you can. I wasted half my life being angry, and it only hurt me in the end."

"I need some time."

"I get that. Take some time. Just don't take the rest of your life, okay?"

She nods, and I sense it's time for me to go, so I stand up.

"Thanks, Ms. Romano."

"Anytime," I say.

And I go on my way.

———

Dan and I have been living in denial, not talking about what the future holds, and that's fine with me. I'm walking over to his place now. He said he had some news for me. I'm glad I didn't need to blow his cover that night, because it seems like he's making some progress on his case. I think that might mean it's coming to an end.

I wonder what that means in terms of his teaching job here. Will they let him finish out the semester, or will they just pull him? I always knew this could happen, so I'm trying to brace myself. I swore I'd never let my life be defined by a guy again. I've learned my lesson, and I'm prepared for whatever happens.

"Hey," he says as I enter, and he gives me a peck on the lips.

"Hey back. What's up?"

"I have some news. Regarding my assignment."

"Are you telling me as your boss or as the woman you're fooling around with?"

"Is that what we're doing? Fooling around?" He pushes my hair back from my face and we enjoy a long, lingering kiss. It sets my body on fire, but I want to finish this conversation.

"Hold on, Romeo. What's the word?"

He takes a step back and runs his hand through his hair. He's stalling.

"Just spit it out," I say.

"I'm moving on in two weeks."

I'd be lying if I said his words didn't feel like a gut punch, but I'm not sure if it's because I'll have to get through the rest of the semester alone, here in the Arctic Circle, or if I'm feeling something more than simply lust for him.

"And I bet you can't even tell me where you're going."

"Actually, I can. That's my other news. I'm getting out of undercover work and taking a desk job in another field office."

"Really? And why is that?"

He pulls me in again and strokes my hair.

"Because I realized what I was missing. It's so hard, trying to be with someone when you can't even tell them who you really are. I've hurt my share of women. And that's the few times I've even allowed myself more than a casual hookup. I don't want to do that again. What we experienced made me see what I was missing. And I meant it when I said I didn't want to cause you any more pain."

It occurs to me that what I've been feeling for Dan might not be love. It could simply be the fact that I can be myself around him and that might be mutual, although I'm not sure that's dawned on him.

"So, where are you going?"

"Albuquerque. An SSA position opened up. Supervisory special agent. It's a promotion of sorts."

I laugh out loud. "You're kidding me!"

"No. Why?"

"That's one of the places I want to visit on my drive back to California. I have the trip all mapped out."

"You don't say!"

"I do say. And congratulations on the promotion."

"So this place hasn't grown on you? You're outta here in June?"

"I'm counting the days until I can pack my car and go. Especially after that blizzard insanity. If I never see another snowflake again, it'll be too soon."

"I'll have to wait until summer to see you? That seems long."

This catches me by surprise.

"You can come visit me," I say.

"I could fly you out to see me on your spring break."

"We'll see. I owe my friend in Florida a visit. I've already got the tickets."

As we go over the logistics of managing what could be my first long-distance relationship, it becomes clear to me that I'm not ready to make that kind of commitment. As hunky as Dan is, I don't want to rush into anything. We don't know each other very well; it was circumstances that threw us together. And now that he'll be free from the burden of concealing his identity, he might not want to put all his eggs in my basket, either.

Truthfully, I'm a little jealous. He's free, and I'm still stuck in deep cover mode. I tell him all of this, and his puppy dog eyes look sad. I don't like disappointing him, but it feels good to be in control of my emotions.

I wonder what's changed since my last relationship. I sure feel a lot more for Dan both physically and emotionally than I ever did for Evan, but the thought of him leaving isn't sending me into a tailspin. Perhaps it has something to do with starting to heal my childhood wounds. I meant what I said to Erin, and I hope she takes my advice.

Meanwhile, I pull him in for a kiss.

"You sure about this?" He asks. "We can cool it. No pressure."

"Take off your shirt," I reply, "and I'll let you know."

I might not be sure where I want this relationship to go in the long run, but I know what I want right now.

He flashes me a sly smile, lifts his shirt over his head, and tosses it aside. I run my hands over his muscular shoulders and admire his six-pack abs.

"Yep." I caress his cheek. "I'm sure."

"So unfair! If I ever said something like that to you, you'd—"

"I'd what?" I kiss him. "I wouldn't care at all."

"Okay then. Take off your shirt," he says.

And I do.

———

I'm awakened by the sound of my special ringtone, and my heart is immediately in my throat. My pulse is racing like crazy because it's my mom's ringtone, and it only rings through at this time of night if she's called multiple times.

Something is terribly wrong.

For a moment, I'm disoriented. I'm in Dan's room and it's dark. It takes me a few tries to find my phone on the unfamiliar nightstand.

I pick up.

"Cassie?" Her voice is barely audible.

"Mom? What's wrong?"

"It's your father."

She doesn't need to say anything more. I can tell by the din in the background that she's at the hospital, and judging from her tone, it's not good news. I hold my breath, hoping that after all this time, it's nothing to do with his former associates, that he didn't lose his life at their hands. That they haven't done something horrible to him. That our disappearance wasn't for nothing.

"He had another heart attack," she says. "And he didn't…" Then she chokes up and starts to sob.

I barely notice Dan's hand on my shoulder as I crumble into myself. It's not like with Kimi when it took me a bit to process the news. This hits me all at once like a tidal wave, and I can barely breathe as I try to gulp in air between sobs. I let out all the pent-up tension from the last couple of weeks.

And then my sobs slow to a trickle as I move on to reflect on the tender memories of my dad and me in my childhood. Over Christmas, my father and I finally got back to that comfortable place, and I know I should be grateful for that. But I'm not. I'm angry. At myself, for waiting so long. And at the world, for the sheer injustice of it all.

After a bit, Mom and I both pull it together. She has to go, she says, there's a lot to take care of.

"I'll be home as soon as I can, Mom," I say.

And I get to work finding flights.

THIRTY-SIX

Cassie

My father's services were surprisingly comforting, and although the past two weeks have been very difficult for me, I'm headed in the right direction. We were able to loosen up the rules a bit and invite relatives we haven't seen in a while to the service. It was comfortable and warm, and although it was a sad occasion, it was nice to be part of a larger family again. Everyone shared stories of my irascible and charming dad and his many adventures.

We're still technically in WITSEC, but only as an extreme precaution. I feel like a weight has been lifted off me now that a slip of the lip won't bring our whole family down or lead to someone finding my dad. I feel as if I've been holding my breath since I was thirteen, and I can finally let it out.

I'm not really worried about my personal safety anymore. The whole point of going after either of us would be to cause my dad pain, and you can't hurt a dead man, which is something Dan pointed out before I left for California.

And although there's a part of me that's relieved, the relief is tempered by the extreme sadness of knowing that I'll never see my dad again. Time, I suppose, will help heal the pain, and I'm finally feeling grateful that we spent his last Christmas together in Manhattan.

I had a good talk with my mother while I was home, and I feel closer to her now. The abrupt move all those years ago was hard on her too, but she stuck with him through it all. They were really in love, and I guess that's something I've taken for granted all my life, being raised by two parents who loved each other. In spite of everything, it was a good marriage, and I can tell she's hurting deeply.

"Do you believe him?" I asked.

"About?"

"That he didn't know the merchandise was stolen."

She took a deep breath. "People see what they want to see," she said.

"And what do you think?"

"I took him at his word," she said. "It was the crowd he ran in. The way he grew up. His associates were harmless, Cassie. He never meant for any of this to happen. And he certainly didn't mean to get mixed up with any terrorist cell."

"Do you think we were ever in real danger?"

"No. Not really. His cronies were too low level, and he gave up little of value to the authorities. But it was the right move to get a new start. His reputation was effectively trashed, so starting over was the best option. For us. Maybe not for you."

"It's okay, Mom. I get it now."

Then she switched gears.

"I have some good news for you."

"Good news?"

"Yes, hold on a minute. I need to get something from the den."

I hear a knock at my apartment door, and I know who it is. It's Sunday morning, and Dan's leaving today. I'm sad because I know I'll be lonely, but I have Ed, and he needs me. He's still having a hard time processing the fact that he shot someone, and I have a feeling he might retire after this year.

I'm still not ready to make a commitment to a long-distance relationship though, especially since I don't know what I'm doing with my career, but I'm also not ready to lose Dan forever. It's only February, and we don't want to wait until June to see each other again. I'm sticking with my plan to go to Florida for spring break, so we decided that he'll come here for a long weekend in mid-April, and we'll do a staycation in Manhattan.

I'm not sure how that will feel, with the bittersweet memories of my last days with my dad still fresh in my mind. I can't imagine never going there again, though, so I figure it's better to get it over with sooner rather than later.

I open the door, and he steps inside.

"I'm all packed up," he says.

Our last night together was perfect, so there's not much more to say. He never revealed his cover to anyone but me, Doug Walker, and whoever knew on the board, so most people think he's a total flake who's left two teaching positions in the last three months. He gave "family issues" as his excuse this time, and nobody asked questions, but there were a fair number of eye rolls.

I was able to fill his position with someone Doug recommended, a woman he knew from a previous job whose husband was recently transferred to a position in Westchester, about an hour south of here. A part of me wonders if she's some sort of undercover agent too, but I don't dare ask. I've had enough intrigue for one year, and the dirty donor investigation is of no consequence to me, so I'll stay out of it.

We steal one last kiss before we step outside my door. Then I walk down with him to his car. He doesn't have much stuff, and I have no idea if he's driving to Albuquerque or if he's dropping the car off at some federal installation and flying home. He said he'll call me when he "gets settled," whatever that means.

"I'll see you around," I say as he gets behind the wheel.

"Right back atcha, Romano," he replies.

Then I blow him a kiss.

He smiles. Then he starts up the car, waves one last time out the car window, and drives away.

THIRTY-SEVEN

Cassie

"**H**ow're you feeling?" Ed asks as I plop down with my breakfast tray. "You've sure been through a lot these last few weeks."

I don't normally eat breakfast in the cafeteria. I missed dinner last night, though, and I'm really hungry. I got through Sunday night just fine, but I wasn't in the mood to deal with people. I'm not looking forward to onboarding a new teacher this week, but aside from that, all is well.

"I could say the same about you. How are you?"

"I asked you first."

"I'm…fine."

"First your dad and now Dan? How can you be fine?"

"Dan? You think I'm falling apart because I lost an English teacher?" I offer him a wry smile.

"Oh, come on. I know you guys were knocking boots."

"Are you speaking as my friend or as my boss who could fire me for something like that?"

"I'm speaking as your boss who, I believe, suggested that you go for it. Was that a mistake? I hope he didn't hurt you."

231

"Okay, if you must know, it was good advice. He didn't hurt me. And we've decided to keep in touch. He's planning to come visit me in April, and I'm going to see him on my drive back to California in June."

"Drive back to where? Visit from...where?" His brow furrows. "I thought he was from around here."

I feel my heart start to race and my eyes widen.

Shit!

Ed has a sly grin on his face now. "Don't worry, Cassie. Doug Walker read me in. I know who he is."

"That was...Ed! What the hell?"

"But seriously, Cass, you need to do better at keeping this under wraps. Doug and I are the only ones who know."

If you only knew how much I've kept under wraps.

"Don't worry, Ed. I can think on my feet."

"So, you're not staying on next year?"

"Of course not. What about you?" I ask.

"I'm planning to retire. Doug knows, but he doesn't want to announce it just yet, so keep that under wraps. I was thinking you might like to go for the dean of faculty position. It pays a lot, and it'd be great experience."

"Not if my life depended on it."

And then I smile, thinking about the fact that I can pretty much do whatever I want with my life now, within reason. Although I've been through a lot the last few months, I'm in a better place now than I was when I arrived. Emotionally, of course. But also financially. And it's nice to know I can ride out the rest of the year with one person who actually knows some of my secrets.

"You planning to drive cross-country?"

"Yes! I have it all planned out."

"Me too. I'm planning to leave in early July. I told Doug that's as long as I can stay. And then I'll road-trip around to see some friends and family," he says.

Ed's done the cross-country trip many times with his wife in a camper, and his face lights up as he whips out his phone and starts making suggestions to me while we compare notes about our plans. We continue like this for a long while, both of us excited about our futures, and it feels great.

I glance over and see Erin Kensington sitting with Marko, the Ukrainian student she was paired with in the buddy program. They seem like more than buddies to me. There's a glow about her, and they're leaning in close.

I smile at this and the fact that life goes on, for all of us, whether we want it to or not. It seems as if she'll be fine. Things could have been worse for both of us. We were both raised by parents who loved us, which is more than some people can say.

I'm looking forward instead of backward for the first time in a long while, focusing on the positives and relishing the fact that I'm in control of my life for once. Maybe I always was, but I just couldn't see it.

It doesn't hurt that my dad had a rather large life insurance policy. When my mother handed me the check that day, my eyes nearly popped out of my head. I'm not a multimillionaire or anything, but it's a nice chunk of change. Enough to purchase a modest condo in cash and then some.

I can only hope my dad knows how much I loved him, and that I forgive him. I never had the chance to say that to him, and it's my only regret. So I look up towards the sky and say it to him now.

I forgive you, Dad.

I see him smile. *Forget about it, Cass. We're good*, he says. And we are.

EPILOGUE

Madeline
Three months later

I've adjusted as well as I can to prison life. It's not a minimum-security facility, like the ones where white-collar criminals do their time. We're not sitting around folding origami. But it could be worse.

They gave me fifteen to twenty as part of my plea deal, and there's always the chance I can get time off for good behavior. I'm a model prisoner, and I've become a celebrity of sorts around here. Well, maybe not a celebrity. More like a valuable resource for the other inmates.

When word got out that I'd been able to secure a relatively light sentence for murder, women started coming to me for advice. Then I took a job in the prison library. Not many people in here have my level of education, so it wasn't too hard to secure. I started helping some of the other prisoners to research legal strategies for their cases. Most of them claim they're innocent, and I'm sure the majority are full of shit, but I did help one woman who I know for certain got a raw deal.

She shot her abusive husband after he nearly cracked her head open with a tire iron, and I'd always assumed those cases were slam dunks for an acquittal based on self-defense. But this one wasn't, and I took a special interest in her case. I can't stand wife beaters. I went over her defense and found all kinds of issues. Then I hooked her up with the Innocence Project, and she's currently planning an appeal strategy.

Even if most of these women I counsel will never see the inside of a courtroom again, the fact that I have this skill offers me a measure of protection. I'm worth more to them alive than dead, so I don't see what any of them would gain by killing me.

Speaking of being killed, although I'm not really worried about a beef with the women in here, I am concerned about what someone outside these walls might pay one of them to do to me. I know a great deal more than my husband about the "questionable" large donations that were made to the school. I have a pipeline of sorts from my younger days, and I thought if Miles brought in big money, we'd be able to leverage that success and improve our social standing.

That obviously didn't happen, and I wasn't stupid enough to give any of them up. I gave up Butch MacDonald instead because he's the one who profited the most from all of this, although he always cut me a small finder's fee that I tucked away in my private slush fund, for Erin. He appears to have left the country, and nobody's been able to locate him, so I don't see why he'd rock the boat. But then you never know.

On the walk from the library to my cell I turn the corner and almost run smack into an inmate I don't recognize.

She must be new.

I'm about to go around her when I see the focused look in her eye and catch the glint of the knife blade she holds in her hand. I close my eyes and accept my fate, comforted by the knowledge that my daughter will be well taken care of, and not just because of my slush fund. I changed the beneficiary on my life insurance policy. My only regret at the moment is that I won't be around to see the look on my husband's face when he finds out he gets nothing.

Cassie
One year later

I landed at a small private day school in Scottsdale, Arizona, where I'm the new assistant principal. It turned out my mom was sick of the cold too, and she wanted to be closer to her relatives in Nevada now that she's free to interact with them more often. I wasn't interested in going back to the Vegas area, so we compromised on Arizona. I've always loved the desert, but I wanted something a bit more mountainous than where I grew up. Maybe the Catskills grew on me. I still won't be caught dead on top of a mountain in winter, though.

My mom bought a nice three-bedroom home in a retirement community about twenty minutes from me, and she's having a blast meeting new people and being social. I purchased a two-bedroom townhome in North Scottsdale, which I'm loving.

As for Dan, he's living just outside Albuquerque, and we see each other most weekends. I like going there to visit, but Arizona suits me better overall. If things work out between us and we want to take it to the next level, he can always transfer to one of the Phoenix offices. For now, this is working out just fine.

We've met each other's families, and my mother adores him. He's from a big family who all live near him, so my mother and I spent Christmas with his entire extended family. He's fluent in Spanish—his mother's side's bilingual—and I feel like an idiot when I hear him switch effortlessly from one language to the other. I'm horrible at anything besides English. Now he's trying to teach me Spanish, and I'm hopeless. He keeps trying, refusing to give up on me.

I heard from Erin a few times after I left but not recently. The last time was mid-October when she was first away at college and likely feeling a bit homesick. She reached out to me and I answered her, but she didn't reply to my email asking how she was doing, so I assume she's adjusted to college life. I attended her mother's funeral, and her father thanked me for the support I provided. I didn't feel I'd done much of anything, and I'm frankly surprised Erin even mentioned me to him. He's not in prison, and that's about all I know.

I wonder still about her head case of a mother and what was going through that mind of hers that night. Did she just snap? Or was she always a psycho waiting to happen? At least she can't harm anyone now, and I feel good that I'm finally in the clear.

I'm coming back from a trail walk near my place, headed into my local coffee shop, when a man reaches the door before me and holds it open. He looks familiar, but I can't quite place him. He's probably in his mid-sixties, and he's wearing sunglasses and a hat.

"Thanks," I say and walk through the door ahead of him.

He looks around, like he's meeting someone.

"Hey, Bill!" a woman calls out from a table near the plate glass window that overlooks the sidewalk. He nods and walks over to her. As he approaches the table, he takes off his hat and glasses, and my heart skips a beat.

It's Butch MacDonald. Or is it?

I turn away and rush over to the coffee line. I could swear I saw a resemblance, but then I only got a quick look, and I don't want to call attention to myself by glancing in his direction again. If it is him, I don't want him to notice me.

We've only met once, when I interviewed at Falcon Ridge nearly two years ago, so I doubt he would even have a clue who I am. His portrait still hangs in the halls there, so I have the advantage.

Could it be him?

I decide that I don't want to know. My mind is probably playing tricks on me. I still have nightmares about Madeline Kensington finding me in that closet, and in them, things don't turn out so well for me. It's probably just some kind of PTSD.

I should probably see a therapist.

I tell myself it's not him. And if by some strange twist of fate, WITSEC relocated him here after he gave up some dirty donors, I don't want to know about it. So I forgo the coffee, do an about-face, and walk out the door.

But as I walk past the café window, I can't help but sneak one last glance at their table. Our eyes meet through the glass and his brows rise.

And he winks at me.

ACKNOWLEDGEMENTS

I would like to extend my sincere thanks to the many people who helped me craft this novel. Thanks goes out once again to my husband who brainstormed with me endlessly when I hit plot challenges and who also read countless drafts of my manuscript. He has a wealth of knowledge in the genre and a great eye for detail. Although he thinks otherwise, I could not have put out so many well received novels without his assistance.

Thanks to my invaluable alpha readers Robin, Susan, and Donna who offered great suggestions and encouragement. Thanks to my chief beta reader Christina Yother at Your Beta Reader, whose suggestions and attention to detail went way beyond a typical beta read, offering valuable ideas to make the manuscript better. As always, thanks to my fabulous editor Julie MacKenzie for her expert attention to detail and timely delivery of her editorial comments and corrections.

Thanks to all of my stellar educational coworkers, school administrators, and students for a rewarding career that has sustained my interest throughout the decades. I'm fortunate to have worked at three fabulous independent schools over the course of my career which, thankfully, were nothing like Falcon Ridge Academy. Thanks to the ALICE active shooter training program that provided us with some tools to protect ourselves and our students.

Finally, thanks so much to my readers. You are why I keep writing, and I am so grateful for the time you take to read my books as well as rate and review them. I read all of my reviews and it helps me to improve, so please keep them coming. I really appreciate it. I'm presently working on a stand-alone sequel to *The Stepfamily* which should be out sometime early next year. For more information on new releases and specials, please go to www.bonnietraymore.com.

ABOUT THE AUTHOR

Bonnie Traymore is the author of several recent domestic thriller novels. Originally from the New York City area, she's lived in Honolulu with her family for the last few decades. When she's not writing, she enjoys being in the classroom with young minds, keeping her work fresh and current. She's also an accomplished non-fiction writer, historian, and veteran educator with a doctorate in United States History. She has taught at top independent schools in Honolulu, Silicon Valley, and New York City, and she's taught history courses at Columbia University and the University of Hawai'i.

Please enjoy a sample of
The Stepfamily: A Psychological Thriller,
Book 1, Silicon Valley Series.

PROLOGUE

Three months ago

She stands in silence, reading the weathered letter she holds in her trembling hands—over and over and over. A rage simmers deep inside her, about to erupt as she grasps the implications. Yet it all makes perfect sense for her now. The pieces of her life that never quite fit together suddenly snap into place as the truth reveals itself to her.

Her entire life, she now realizes, has been a lie. A fraud. A fractured fairy tale. How can anyone be expected to turn a blind eye to that kind of realization? How can anyone forgive that level of deception?

She's trying to hold it together, she really is, but the feeling bubbling up inside her is too powerful to suppress. It washes over her like a tidal wave, and suddenly she's willing to risk everything to get what she needs—and eliminate anyone who stands in her way.

ONE

I've never felt at home in this family because it's not really mine. But I try. Why? I don't really know. I could speak up. I could protest. I could leave. But I don't.

My husband is tenser than usual this morning. I can see it in his jawline when he walks into the kitchen.

"How's the approval coming?" I ask.

"Oh, you know, the usual hurdles. Nothing to worry about," he replies. He tries to hide it, but his discomfort breaks through. His voice is a little singsongy, always a sign that something's up.

He walks over to the coffee pot, pours himself a cup, and pops a slice of bread in the toaster. A dark blue tie hangs loose around his neck. He never wears one. Hardly anyone in Silicon Valley does, so it must be an important day. But for some reason, I don't think his unease has anything to do with work.

"Got a big meeting today?" I ask.

"The board wants an update," Peter replies.

"Aren't you just waiting for the FDA?"

"Yeah."

"So, isn't that the update?"

"Yeah." He smiles. "But you know how they are."

Then he shrugs, and I smile back. He butters his toast and pours some more coffee into a travel mug. I can tell that's all I'm going to get out of him. He's a calm man—most of the time. But he does have a temper, and even after twelve years, I still can't tell what might set it off. I can tell he's stressed, so I leave it alone.

I watch him walk over to the large beveled mirror that hangs in our dining room. He fastens his tie in one fluid motion. It looks sexy. Masculine. Commanding. The way he snaps it up and down at same time to force it into compliance. He's older than me, but he still gets my heart racing with his salt-and-pepper hair and chiseled physique. His sleeves are rolled up a bit, exposing his muscular forearms.

He walks back to the kitchen and wolfs down his toast. Standing at the island countertop, I continue to make a veggie sandwich to pack for lunch. He places his dish in the sink behind me. We don't speak. It's a comfortable silence, but I can't shake the feeling that something is up.

I turn around to face him. "Well, I'm sure you'll dazzle them." I smile and rest my hand on Peter's bicep. I run my thumb across its taut surface.

"I don't know about that." He places his hand on my shoulder, leans over, and gives me a peck on the lips. "Have a good day." Then he grabs his coffee and heads out the side door to the garage.

I hear his car start and the garage door rise up. We have a two-car garage, but there's only space for one car because he's got all kinds of tools and sports equipment that take up the other half. It was like that when we started dating. Only one car in the garage. Twelve years later, my car still sits in the driveway.

I don't belong here. I'm still a visitor. Just like my car.

I'm searching through my clothes rack, second-guessing myself once again. I turn to look at myself in the full-length mirror that hangs on the opposite side of my closet. My navy skirt sits just above the knee, and I worry that people might think I'm playing up my sexy legs. But I'm not. It's just how my legs look. I don't want to wear pants. My blouse is modest, and I tell myself to stop being so insecure. I pull out a few different pairs of shoes from the cubbies and try them on. I land on strappy sandals with a medium heel. They're dark, almost the same color as my hair. I look professional but in a confident, sexy way. It's fine.

I have a big day today too. My career is really taking off. Finally. I was so young when I met Peter. Only twenty-seven. I'd just finished graduate school, a marketing MBA, and at first, there was too much going on in our lives to do much of anything with it. But I've made up for lost time. And I recently got a big promotion. Laura Sato Foster, Vice President of Monetization. Is that what's making him uncomfortable? The fact that I might not need him anymore? He's always been a big supporter of my career. It can't be that. But something is bothering him, that's for sure. He even rejected my advances last night, which he's never done before. He just turned fifty, and I hope it's not a sign of what's to come.

I make my way downstairs and out the front door to the driveway where my car sits. It's a silver Audi A6, so it's not an over-the-top choice, especially for this area, but it's certainly garage-worthy. I plop my satchel in the trunk, and then I notice something. A small stream of fluid is running out from under the car. We live in Los Altos Hills near the top of a long road—a very winding and steep one. Our driveway also slants down a bit; otherwise, I don't think I would have noticed the fluid. Thank goodness for gravity.

I'm a bit neurotic, the kind of person who runs back into the house to make sure the stove is off. I always pump my brakes before I back out of the driveway. Losing brakes on a hill like the one we live on could be fatal, and while that trickle of liquid could be anything, I have a sinking feeling in my stomach.

I open the car door and get behind the wheel. I press the start button and see the brake indicator light up. Then I step hard on the brake pedal. There's a slight resistance at first, but then my foot sinks to the floor. I realize then that it must be the brake fluid—one of my biggest fears. I feel a strange tingling in the back of my head.

I try not to catastrophize, but it's a pretty new car, although it's due to be serviced. Do brake lines start leaking for no reason? Probably not. Even before I call for help, I know this isn't good, and my stomach lurches as I consider the implications. It's quite possible that someone has tampered with my brake line.

Someone who's out to get me?

―――――

Peter's seated at the mahogany conference table at work, but his mind is a mile away. He's trying to forget about the email he found in his spam folder the other day, but it gnaws at him like a tick burrowing into his ankle flesh.

"*Peter?* Are you with us?" the chairman barks.

"Yes!" Peter snaps back into reality. He knows he has to get his head in the game, but he's missed the question completely, so there's no way he can fake it. He can get away with something like that once but not a second time, so he forces himself to focus.

"George asked if you have any concerns about what Sahil's team found when they tried to reproduce the results for the lung cancer experiments." It was the CEO, repeating the chairman's question.

"Sorry, I was looking over the FDA's last response. Yes, of course I have concerns."

"What do you plan to do about it?"

"We've already started on another round of experiments. I'm sure it was their mistake. We've performed those experiments numerous times for the study. They've only done it once, so I wouldn't worry just yet."

"We've already released that data in a preprint," the chairman says. "You better hope it was their mistake."

"Give me a week, okay?"

Everyone nods in agreement. Nobody wants this to be an issue, especially with a lucrative merger and FDA approval of their drug on the horizon. It will be fine. The data is good, he tells himself.

And even if it's not, it's the least of his worries right now.

———

"You look rattled. Is everything okay?" My assistant, Mina, looks up at me as I go rushing past her desk and into my office twenty minutes before my first important meeting as the new Vice President of Monetization—and two hours later than normal.

"Car trouble. I had to take an Uber," I call out to her and duck into my office. I wasn't about to tell anyone at work about the brake line. What if it was one of them?

Mina pokes her head in my door as I toss my half-opened satchel on my desk, spilling the contents onto the surface.

"Car trouble?" She's eyeing me with a curious look, hands on her hips, her dark hair cascading down the front of her tan sweater dress. She seems to sense that something's up, although it's hard to tell with her. She's got these mysterious coal eyes, the eyes of an old soul, with lashes so long they look fake, but she swears they're not. I'd kill for lashes like that.

"Car trouble!" I widen my eyes and shrug to let her know we're moving on. We've had a friendship of sorts over the years, although she's quite a bit younger than me. But now that she's working directly for me, I've had to pull back a bit.

"Do you need anything for the meeting?" she asks.

I smile. "No, I'm good, thanks. Just a few minutes to collect my thoughts." She's a great assistant. I consider telling her about my car, but there's no time.

"I'll leave you to it then." She exits, and I decide I'll probably fill her in on the brake incident later. After I've had time to process it. If there's anyone I can trust around here, it's her.

The mechanic who came out to the house confirmed what I'd suspected. The rubber brake hose had been severed, but he couldn't say for sure that it had been tampered with. It's apparently hard to prove something like that. Sometimes road debris—a sharp rock, for example—could damage it enough to weaken it, and then it could simply rupture. And there's plenty of road debris where I live. I'm looking at a photo taken by the mechanic. There's a smoother-looking break on one side, and then it's ragged on the other like it tore apart. He also said that extreme heat could wear down the rubber more quickly, and we've certainly had our share of that this summer. But I'm not convinced by his road debris theory.

Instead of preparing for my meeting, I Google "brake line cut" and discover that there have been isolated pockets of this sort of vandalism in various communities across the country recently. Phoenix. Denver. The Seattle area. They've all been hit. I play a few videos of news broadcasts and listen to frantic residents recount their stories. Like me, at first, they thought that someone was out to get them until a pattern emerged. Who would want to cut the brake hoses of a bunch of strangers? No arrests have been made in any of the cases so far. Although it's a terrifying thought, that a random vandal is targeting my neighborhood, I suppose it's better than the idea that someone is out to get me specifically. I'll go to the police station and file a report. Right after my meeting.

"Laura?" It's my boss at my office door.

I finally have an office, and I thought it would be great. But it doesn't give me as much privacy as you might expect. Nobody closes their door around here. We're technically allowed to work from home if we want, but it's starting to feel like a bad career move if you actually do it.

"Hi, Bethany."

She's the CFO, and I report to her. It's my job to figure out how to start making money. We're venture-capital funded, like many startups in Silicon Valley, and the funding is drying up for this round. I'm supposed to have ideas about how to monetize our product. That's what they pay me for. I've got a few, and I'm sure they're terrible. But maybe that's how everyone feels. We're all just grasping at straws here.

"Are you ready for the meeting?"

"Sure."

"I'm counting on you, Laura. I went out on a limb for you." She holds up a finger, her eyebrows raised high above her translucent hazel eyes as they peer at me, boring into my skull. They look a little unsettling, framed by her wild red hair, which is especially unruly today. "Don't screw this up."

I nod, and she goes on her way. Nobody tells you this, but the gloves come off the closer to the top you get. All the polite formalities and HR-sponsored platitudes fall by the wayside. And what if I do screw up? Then it's game over. I'm out.

People would kill for an opportunity like this, Bethany said, when she told me I'd gotten the promotion.

But they wouldn't.

Would they?

TWO

A police officer sits across from me at our imposing dining room table. It's pretentious and formal—not my style—and I feel awkward sitting so far away from him. I would have rather sat in the living room, but this is where he sat. The officer is about forty, with a few extra pounds on his large frame. He seems less than enthused with the assignment. I decided to have the authorities meet me at home so the police could have a look at the car before it got towed in. I was too flustered earlier to make a decision about what to do. After the mechanic came and told me it was the brake line—or, more specifically, the right front brake hose—I told him to leave it there and hopped into an Uber to get to work for my meeting.

"So, what time did you go out to your car, again?"

"About eight thirty this morning," I repeat.

We've already been over this. Why is he asking me again? I can't tell if he's actually concerned about the possibility of a neighborhood vandal or if he's humoring me. He did inform me that the department has been on the lookout for this sort of thing based on warnings from other municipalities. But then he assured me that, as far as he knew, the Bay Area had so far been spared. I worry now that he'll think I'm paranoid if I ask him to dig further.

"And there's nothing on your security camera?"

"No. I have a pretty clear shot of the driveway from one of the cameras, and I didn't see anyone tampering with my car."

"The break is pretty jagged, at least on one side, based on these photos, so my best guess is that it probably got sliced by some road debris that got up into it like your mechanic suggested. Then it wore down and broke."

"Or someone could have cut it in another location," I say.

"True, but then they didn't do a very good job. That would mean they didn't know enough to cut it all the way."

"Maybe they got interrupted. Or wanted to make sure my brakes went while I was driving."

"Could be. But you'd probably have noticed it on your way home."

"The mechanic said it might take a few miles to notice if it was a small cut to begin with."

The officer nods. I can tell he thinks I'm being paranoid. I consider asking him to dust for prints, but since he doesn't bring it up, I assume it would be an inappropriate suggestion. The mechanic's prints are probably all over it anyway. And if someone was trying to kill me, wouldn't they be smart enough to wear gloves?

I hear a car pull up to the house and wonder who it could be. This doesn't seem like it would warrant another officer. The car stops in the driveway, and I hear a door slam. Then I hear someone running.

What the hell?

I stand up, and so does the officer.

A moment later, Peter comes bursting through the doorway. He runs up to me before I can react or say anything.

"What's happening?" Peter's face is pale, as if he's seen a ghost. I can see sweat beads forming, about to drip from his temples. I should have called to tell him about this, but I knew he had an important meeting. I didn't want to worry him until I knew more. But what is he doing home so early? It's only three in the afternoon.

After my meeting, which went swimmingly, I told Bethany about my car, and she encouraged me to go handle it. She's a hard-ass when it comes to work, but she's not a monster, and she seemed genuinely concerned. More than the officer standing next to me but much less so than my husband, who looks like he's about to have a stroke.

He takes my face in his hands. "Laura? Are you alright?"

"I'm fine, Peter."

"What's going on? Why didn't you call me?" My husband is frantic, and I don't get it. I'm obviously fine.

"Everything's okay, Mr. Foster," the officer informs him. "Please. Have a seat."

So we sit down and take Peter through the whole story from the beginning. I'm much more of a worrier than my husband is, so I expect him to brush it off. And he does, on the surface. But I can tell he's faking it. And I don't have a clue as to why.

"Well, Laura, if there's nothing on the security camera, I'd say it's pretty safe to assume that it was an accident," Peter says. But he's addressing the officer, avoiding eye contact with me. His lips are pressed together, and his jaw is tight. I feel like his words are at odds with his body language.

But then maybe his mood has nothing to do with the brake situation. Maybe it's the same issue that was bothering him this morning, and he came home early to talk to me about it. *But how would he know I was here?*

We wrap things up and see the officer to the door. He assures me they will "check into it," but I'm not holding my breath. I close the door behind him.

Then Peter lets out a deep sigh and almost collapses on the floor. He bends over and puts his hands on his knees, taking deep breaths, looking like he might pass out. *Maybe he's not feeling well, and that's why he came home early?*

"Laura, I thought…"

And then it hits me.

The last time a police officer was here, it was to give him some terrible news. He *has* seen a ghost today. The ghost of Cynthia Foster—his college sweetheart, the mother of his children, the woman whose home I inhabit.

I walk over, and he takes me in his arms, holding me close.

"I'm fine, Peter. I'm totally fine." I lean back and smile at him, my hands resting on his arms.

"I love you so much, Laura. If anything ever happened to you…"

"Peter. It's nothing. Really. I'm sure the hose just wore out like the officer said."

I rack my brain, trying to think if there is anything connected to his late wife that could have triggered his tense mood this morning. I watch for signs around the anniversary of her death, but that's months away. And it's gotten better over the years. He's genuinely concerned about me right now; that much is clear.

But then why wouldn't he press the officer to investigate further? He seemed eager to get rid of him. Maybe it's the bad memories. I can't imagine how hard it must be to live in those memories every day. And I still don't have an explanation as to why he's home in the middle of the afternoon.

"What are you doing home so early?"

"Oh, they're doing some minor renovations at the office and it was noisy, so I decided to come home to work."

"How did your meeting go?"

"It was fine. What about yours, hotshot VP? Did you knock 'em dead?" He brushes my cheek with his knuckle.

"Not quite, but they're worth more to me alive anyway." I smile at him.

He pulls me in for a kiss. Not a peck this time, but a deep, passionate one, and it's clear that whatever was bothering him last night has passed. He slips his hand under my skirt and slides it up my leg. Electricity courses through me. We haven't been very spontaneous lately, so this takes us both by surprise.

Then he takes me by the hand and starts to lead me upstairs. I'm not as excited as he is, though, because as we're walking up the stairs, I think about the look on his face when he walked through the door. All those terrible memories here. *Why won't he let go of this place and all it represents?* I love him, and I've tried to be patient, but I've been playing this game for too long. I decide that I have to put my foot down. I can't take a backseat to a ghost forever. We have to sell this place and move on. It's time.

Peter rolls over on his side and watches Laura as she gets out of bed and heads for the shower. Her petite, hourglass figure is a walking work of art. He loves her, and that terrifies him. If anything were to happen to her, well, he doesn't even want to think about that. He tries to keep his cool, but he has a hard time believing that the severed brake line was an accident. It's possible it was random. A neighborhood vandal. But he has a sinking feeling that maybe his past is catching up with him.

Then he tells himself he's being ridiculous. It's all a coincidence. He's letting his imagination get the best of him. It was vandalism. Or a piece of road debris. Regardless, maybe it's a sign that it's time to make a change. Laura's always hated this place. It's dark. And inconvenient, she says. The house isn't all that far from the Los Altos town center in terms of mileage, but it can take forever to wind up and down the hill, especially if you get behind a pack of cyclists, a slow-moving vehicle, or a garbage truck. And they're surrounded by woods. They live in California—one of the sunniest places on earth—yet it's always dark here. And then there's the fire danger, which has increased over the last few years. She never mentions the real reason she wants to move, and he loves her for that. Initially, he told himself he couldn't move because of the kids. But they're out of the house now. What's stopping him? Is it guilt? Maybe, but then he shouldn't punish Laura for his sins.

She comes back into the bedroom wrapped in a pale pink satin robe that sits halfway above her knee. Her dark hair is damp—wet and wild as it falls softly in front of her face—and she looks so sexy.

"What would you think about selling this place? Moving closer to civilization?"

"I thought you'd never ask." She throws off her robe and gets back into bed with him.

THREE

I know I should be thrilled that Peter has finally agreed to sell the house. And I am, for the most part. But I can't shake the feeling there's more to it, and I feel awful about that. There's a logical explanation at my disposal. He panicked when he thought something had happened to me. He realized how much he loves me. And then he decided to give me what I really wanted.

It's a nice explanation, so why doesn't it satisfy me? Is it my natural tendency to be a neurotic worrier, or is it my gut feeling that something is up with him?

Partly, it's because I've never doubted Peter's love for me. I've always felt that his wanting to keep the house had nothing to do with how he feels about me or that he somehow was still in love with his first wife. I've always gotten the feeling their marriage wasn't that great anyway, although he rarely talks about it.

At first, he said it was for the kids. He wanted to honor the memory of their mother. He didn't want to disrupt their lives. But they're pretty much grown now. His son is in his last year of college, and his daughter is in her mid-twenties with a life of her own. They're rarely here these days, although I expect when we tell them, they'll throw a fit. For some reason, they love this dark, desolate home, and they've never totally accepted me as the woman of the house. It's hard enough to come into a family after a divorce. But after a death, it's almost impossible to do anything right.

It's Saturday on a late summer morning that promises to be another scorching hot day, and I'm on my way to meet my triathlon team for a run. I'm late because a pack of amateur cyclists is hogging the road as I start up a rolling hill. I'm driving Peter's SUV, and it's not as nimble as my Audi, which is in the shop. They're riding three or four across, and they're struggling. They should know better. I'm a cyclist. I'd never do that. No wonder people hate us. I feel like honking at them, but I don't.

"Single file, people!" I call out my window to them in a pleasant voice to try to soften the blow. I say it with a smile but not a friendly one. More like a Chucky doll grimace. One woman almost loses her balance as she turns to me. They try to move into a more streamlined formation. I can tell they aren't very experienced. They're a danger to themselves as much as the rest of us.

I finally pass them and continue down the long, winding road, turning left onto Foothill Boulevard, which feels like the autobahn by comparison. Next, I turn off on Alpine, and then it's more winding roads through Woodside to my destination— the parking lot at Windy Hill Preserve. I get to the meeting point a bit late, but if I run fast, I might be able to catch the team. I park my car, grab my water bottle, and head out along the bone-dry trails of Portola Valley.

It's a hill run today, three miles to the top and then a winding five miles or so back down. Not overly long for us in terms of distance, but it's super steep, so it will be a challenging run—just what I need to get my mind off my problems. It's early August, and it's been hot as blazes the past few weeks, so I don't want to push myself too hard in the beginning or I'll run out of steam. We're training for the Santa Cruz Half Ironman in a few weeks, and we're starting to taper.

I'm running a bit faster than usual though, to try to catch the team, and I know it's going to mess up my pacing a bit. But it is nice to be alone with my thoughts, which I let float by. I notice the birds today because the air is still. Their pleasant whistling calls fill the air. *Sweet, sweet. Sweet, sweet.* It's fitting. If sugar had a sound, it would sound like that. I don't have any idea what kind of bird it is, but it's a nice distraction on my run.

I'm in a narrow passage now, and the bird calls have faded. I notice the sound of my own breathing getting heavier as I begin the incline. The gnarled trees form a tunnel over me as I run through it. A faint musty smell lingers in the air. There are patches of wet, mossy green here where the sun doesn't reach, and the Douglas firs and eucalyptus trees show off their verdant hues, but the leaves on the towering oaks look like kindling to me—whisper thin in variegated shades of brown, crumbling on their branches.

My quiet solitude is shattered when I hear someone coming up behind me rather quickly, like they're trying to catch me. It doesn't sound like the pace of a fellow runner. I don't dare to look back, but I suddenly feel very vulnerable all alone in the woods. I can hear their footfalls crunching along the trail. Normally, I wouldn't think twice about it, but today my senses are heightened, and I feel the hairs on the back of my neck stand up. The person is getting closer, and I start to feel panicky. Is someone chasing me?

But that's crazy, I tell myself. It's probably nothing. I think about turning around, but I don't dare. Instead, I run a little faster, trying to get to the open area up ahead. I hear them speed up to match my pace. What if someone did follow me here? Maybe the same person who cut my brake hose. My heart begins to race, so I have to slow down. I try to tell myself it will be okay.

"Laura?" a voice calls out to me. It's a male voice, but I can't quite place it. I turn around and look.

"It's me! Carl!" He's waving. Smiling.

Great. It's this odd guy who used to run with us years ago. He recently moved back to the area and rejoined the team. I'm a bit surprised he recognized me from so far away. And it's especially awkward because he tried to befriend me, but I was a bit reluctant to engage with him. Something about him made me uncomfortable. I have to wait for him, or it will be rude. He's almost caught up to me anyway.

"Hey, Carl!" I wave back as I jog in place.

He's a smaller guy. Very quiet. The kind you see people talking about on the news after he turns out to be a serial killer.

He seemed like such a nice guy. So quiet. So polite.

"Hi, Laura," he says as he jogs up next to me. We continue on the narrow path for a few paces, and soon we come out of the tree tunnel into a flat, open plateau. The Santa Cruz mountains pierce the blue sky, and it feels hotter already.

"Hi, Carl."

"You were really jamming there."

He's a good runner. He's just being polite. I'm out of breath, but he's fine.

"I'm trying to catch up with the others."

We make small talk for a bit as we continue our run, and it's slowing us down. I like running with a big group because you get the camaraderie, but there's no pressure to converse. With one person, it's different. There's this awkward obligation to chitchat. Along the way, he informs me that he's married and has a five-year-old son. I guess it's been a while.

After about a mile, I see a few people from my team stopped ahead of us. They're taking a water break. It's only seven thirty in the morning, and I'm already sweaty. I tell myself I need to get a grip. Carl's a nice guy. A family man. Not a serial killer. *What is wrong with me?*

———

Peter is sitting at the kitchen table in his workout clothes, drenched in sweat. He's just finished a massive cardio session on his Peloton. Laura is out with her triathlon team. Although they both like to keep fit, Peter's more of a gym guy, while she prefers the outdoors. The only time they exercise together is when they're on vacation. If it bothers her at all, she's never let on about it to him.

He pulls up the email again to try to figure out his next move. He hasn't been able to think about much since he read it. He'd discovered it when he was looking for something else in his spam folder the day before yesterday, but it had been sitting there over a week.

I know what you did. I won't tell anyone.

It could be a random spam email. It's pretty generic. He was planning to ignore it, but after what happened to Laura, he feels like he should maybe look into it. There was no call to action, so it probably wasn't a phishing scam. *Don't those usually have a link in them?* He needs to do some research. See if someone can find the IP address.

But how? Maybe he could hire a private detective. *Do they take on cases like this?* And how do you know which ones you can trust? Peter has a window of opportunity while Laura is out, so he starts to do a search. But then he thinks better of it. What if something comes of this, and the authorities take his computer? They'll see he was looking for a private detective. How would that look? He'll have to think of a better way to find one.

In the meantime, he calls the kids and asks them to come over for Sunday dinner. He has to tell them about his decision on the house before he takes any action, and he doesn't expect it to go well. But it's time. He's already told Laura he'd sell, although, in hindsight, he regrets not telling the kids first. Too late for that.

―――――

When I get home from my run, Peter informs me that the children are coming for dinner tomorrow.

"What should I make?"

"Whatever you want."

"Is Lydia still vegetarian?"

"I guess?" He shrugs.

"I'll text the kids and check in with them."

I'm the one who's kept up with all their changing tastes over the years. They were eleven and fourteen when I joined the family. It's hard to believe it when I look at Lydia, but I was around her age when I moved in with them and then married her father, only a year older than she is now. She seems so much younger than that to me. But then I had to mature into my role whether I was ready for it or not. It's the hand I was dealt, falling in love with a widower.

I'm happy that Peter is moving forward on the house sale, but we haven't talked at all about what this might mean. I'm not on the title. And I know the kids view it as their house, although they don't need the money. They have a trust from their mother's side of the family. Peter never had access to it. The bulk of her wealth went directly to the kids through her family's trust when she died, although Peter got the house and their other joint assets. Lydia is twenty-six, so she's started getting her yearly allowance. Carson is still in college, so he doesn't get anything yet, although all of his college expenses are taken care of. We're very fortunate that way.

But what about the house? This is a community property state. And the house should be half mine anyway; I've done enough for this family. But then, he owned it before we got married. One thing for sure is we should talk about it before we tell the kids tomorrow, but I'm at a total loss as to how to bring it up to my husband.

I have only myself to blame for my predicament. I've let myself live so many years in limbo, and now I regret not speaking up sooner. Perhaps we could have moved earlier and saved me all these years of feeling uncomfortable and out of place. But then, it's not really my nature to assert myself. Time flew by, and here I am, in my late thirties, still living in someone else's home. I realize that I need to get over my reticence—at home and at work—and learn to assert myself. The more I live, the more I see that people will eat you alive if you let them. Maybe a cut brake line is exactly what I needed to push me out of my comfort zone.

If you enjoyed this sample, please go to www.bonnietraymore. com for current retail availability.